PEYTON
&
NOAH

PEYTON & NOAH
HEIDI MCLAUGHLIN
© 2018

COVER DESIGN: Sarah Hansen: OkayCreations.
EDITING: My Brother's Editor
EDITING: Ultra Editing Co.

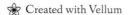 Created with Vellum

To all those who are living their fairytale

PEYTON

*M*y college diploma sits on top of the mantle. I don't know how long I've sat here, staring at it, or how many times I stood in front of it so my fingers could rub over the embossed letters in my name. I'm not sure it's sunk in yet, the fact that I've graduated or the idea that I have job offers waiting to be accepted. It's also one of the last things I have yet to pack for my move to Portland. It's not that I don't want to move, it's that I'm afraid if I box this tangible piece of victory up, the feeling will go away. I achieved another milestone, another win, when doctors all but gave up on me after the accident.

My soon-to-be husband, my lover, my best friend, walks into the living room, carrying two tumblers. Even without tasting the amber colored liquid I know it's my favorite maple crème liqueur from a winery we found while driving through Vermont. The trip to the Northeast was a surprise during spring break. Somehow, Noah knew I needed to get away, that I needed a reprieve from everything that was coming toward me. Finals, graduation, job offers, and the wedding. I smile as he hands me the glass and bring it to my lips. Before taking a sip, I inhale, letting the sweet smell wash over me. Finally, I tip the glass back and close my eyes, letting the flavor bask over my tongue.

"Still gets you every time?" he asks, sitting down next to me.

"I was never a fan of maple until we found that little winery."

"Me neither." Noah reaches for my hand, locking our fingers together. We're never close enough, and yet sometimes we're worlds apart, even when we're sitting right next to each other. Big decisions are weighing heavily on me, on us. Even though he's proposed a Christmas Day wedding, if I take any one of the jobs offered, I'll be asked to work. Being the newbie means I'm one of the lowest employees on the totem pole. They're not going to understand how a quarterback and his sideline reporting fiancée are getting married in the winter. Most of the time I don't understand it, but it's what I want. It's the wedding I envisioned.

We sit in silence, sipping our drinks, while I continue to stare at my degree, and Noah... well, he's just present. Always my constant, my biggest cheerleader, my confidante. He's my reason for being, and deep down I know I came back from the brink of death because of him.

I've never asked what he said to me, but I know he spoke. That much I remember. I tried telling my therapist about my experience, telling her I saw my dad, my grandma and watched my family weep over my body as it lay there, dying. I told her I felt Noah. I felt it every time he touched my leg, my arm or ran his fingers over my bruised cheek. I was there when he cried, when he begged me to stay.

She hasn't come out and told me that I'm making it up or that what I'm describing is only a figment of my imagination, but I sense that's what she thinks. I understand. Death is an unknown. You don't die and come back, at least not often. And those who do, often keep their thoughts to themselves because it's such an odd and unexplainable experience.

The support group I'm in, for people like me, they get it though, and they're helping me come to terms with the memories I have. They've experienced something similar, and most say they altered their path because of it. I didn't, and sometimes I question if I should've. If I had, I wouldn't have to work so hard to avoid the elephant following me around on a daily basis. The amount of pressure I feel to follow my dreams; to be a wife, to become a mother, to be the best friend who helps her guy battle on-the-field demons, wouldn't be weighing me down so much that I want to give up. I wouldn't want to throw my career away before it even starts just so I could be on the sidelines and watch Noah play because I'm so afraid of missing something. Right now, that's the dream I have. To be his constant, his best friend, and his cheerleader. To stand there and cheer my man on. The day I'm asked to critique his game... well, I don't know if I'm going to be able to. Noah expects it. He doesn't want any mercy, and deep down, I don't think I'd show him any but what kind of wife will that make me? What will people say about our relationship? The fact that someone will judge me, judge *us* by what I say, is bothersome.

Noah nuzzles my neck and I lean into him, sighing. He makes everything better, and yet, more complicated. He knows about my memories from when I was in a coma. We spoke at length about me seeing my father and how I wanted to give up. How I wanted to spend just a little more time with him. In my father's world, there is no pain, and in that moment, I was suffering.

"I love you," he whispers against the curve of my neck. Does he know I'm struggling? Can he sense my hesitation? Of course, he can. He's always been in tune with my feelings.

"Am I making a mistake?"

Noah sits up, taking the glass away from my grasp and sets mine and his on the table. Just like that, his mood has changed. He angles himself on the sofa so he can look at me. Brushing my hair behind my ear, his fingers touch one of my scars. It tingles, almost to the point of hurting me. I have dead zones all over, spots where the nerves never reconnected to my system, making them useless and annoying. It's the worst when we're together and I flinch because the man I love touched my side. It scares Noah, breaks his heart. I can see it in his eyes when it happens. He's sorry, and sometimes he's afraid. And I *hate* it.

"Babe, that's a loaded question. Are you making a mistake by moving to Portland? Getting married? Wanting to start a family? Taking a job? What's on your mind?" he asks, cupping my cheek. "Talk to me. I can't help if you keep it bottled up."

When he's like this, it's hard. I'm so in love with him, I just want to curl up and let him take away all my pain, but he's too strong-willed for that. He wants me, no, he demands that I stand on my own two feet, that I be independent, that I strive for greatness. Noah refuses to hold me back, and because of that, I love him unconditionally.

"Marrying you will never be a mistake, Noah Westbury."

He smiles softly. "Thank God because I was starting

to worry."

It's me who's now touching his face, running my fingers over his stubble. "You're the love of my life," I tell him, even though he already knows this.

"Doesn't mean getting married is the right thing to do."

His words shock me. I lean back and look at him questioningly. Is he having second thoughts? Is there doubt in his mind that we're making a mistake? I know I'm young, but I'm ready.

Noah reaches for me, pulling me to his lap, wrapping me in his arms in such a way that I have no choice but to look into his eyes. "I can see the gears spinning, the thoughts cranking away. I know you, Peyton, so I want you to stop. Don't ever question my love for you or look for a hidden message in my words. Your parents aren't married, it works for them. Our wedding date is months away, and we've yet to decide on the simplest things, like a color theme or the flowers. I'm hoping you're doing that with your mom, with Elle, and maybe with my mom and Paige, but if you're not, and this date doesn't work for us, tell me. I'll marry you right now, tomorrow, next year, the year after that, if that's what you want."

"What did I do to deserve a man like you?"

"I ask myself the same question every day about you because you are the love of my life, and I hate that we wasted so many years."

"We needed to grow up."

He laughs. "No, I needed to grow up. You've always been the mature one. Now tell me what's going on?"

I sigh and snuggle into him. If it weren't so hot outside, I'd ask him to build a fire. It's one of the best things about this apartment, the fireplace. When he was able to be here during the season, we often sat here, watching the red, orange, and yellow flames until they flicked out and only embers were left. Noah joked once that we needed a bear skin rug to lay in front of it, so we could make love on it. I laughed, it was a full belly laugh with aching sides, only he wasn't joking. He said men have fantasies too, that don't revolve around Princess Leia.

"What if working isn't the right path for me?"

"Why wouldn't it be?"

I shrug against his chest. "I feel like I've lost so much, even though I haven't, and I don't know if being a career woman is more important than starting a family. What if I take a job and they're not supportive of me taking a week off at Christmas? Still, to this day, the locker room chatter is that wives know better during the season."

"Do you care about what others think?"

"I care about what they say about you. I care about how they'll see me as a professional. It's hard enough for women in this field, and for me to come in and ask for a week off so I can get married...?" I pause and shake my head. "I don't know how that'll go over."

"Who says you have to start this season?"

"No one, but the offers are here now. What if they don't want me next year?"

Noah adjusts the way we're sitting so he can really look at me. His eyes are gentle, almost as if they're pleading with me to let him in. He's in, even if he's having a hard time navigating my thoughts.

"I have a feeling you'll be wanted. You graduated number one in your class. You've had job offers since last summer, they've waited for you for over a year and a half. They can wait a bit longer if you're unsure. And if they can't, then they don't deserve to work with you. Why don't you start after the first of the year? This will give you the freedom to plan our wedding, be with your mom and sister when you need to be."

"And be on the sideline for your games?"

"Babe, I expect you to kick my ass after every game."

I work my body around so that I can straddle Noah. His hands go to my hips. I bear down on him, hoping to feel his need through the flimsy material of my shorts. "What if I tell you that I want to start a family before we're married?"

"I'd carry you to our bedroom and see what I could do about making that happen."

I look over my shoulder toward the direction of our room. Boxes are stacked on top of one another, taped shut, and ready for the movers who are arriving tomorrow. Noah and I have been living out of our suitcases, which honestly isn't out of the ordinary for us. We travel everywhere, between Chicago, Portland, Beaumont, and Los Angeles. I'm surprised we don't just live on a plane. It would make things a hell of a lot easier.

"You don't want to wait until we're married?"

"To make love to you? No," he says, shaking his head wildly and laughing. "To make a baby with you, definitely not because I know how you feel about me, and you know how I feel about you. And someday, whether it's tomorrow, Christmas Day or next year, we're going to take our vows in front of our friends and family, and if that means we have a little one there to watch, so be it."

"You're too good to me."

He brushes my hair off my shoulder, drops his hands to pick me up. "I'm good *because* of you, Peyton. Without you, I am nothing."

2

NOAH

I have never been able to sleep on commercial planes. I don't know if it's the rumbling from the engine, the stagnant air, the uncomfortable seats, or that I've been spoiled by the fact my family has a private jet at their disposal. Still, I try to find some shut-eye on our flight to Portland. Every so often, I open my eyes to look at Peyton. She's deep in thought, scribbling on sticky notes and placing them at the top of the page of her magazine.

"That one's pretty," I tell her, pointing to the dress on the page. She looks at me, smiles, and turns back to the stack sitting on the tray. She pulls one out from the middle and flips it open.

"I was thinking that maybe you could wear a suit instead of a tuxedo."

"Why?"

"Because everyone is always dressed up, either for some gala or the Grammy's, and I thought you, Quinn, the dads, and whoever you ask to stand next to you would like a one-day reprieve."

Despite the console between us, I pull her to me. Her magazine falls to the floor as our lips crash together. "Have I told you how much I love you?"

She nods and kisses me again. "So much," she says before pulling away and adjusting the way she's sitting in her seat.

"Every damn day of my life," I remind her. "And I love that you're thinking about our comfort. I like that suit."

"Me too."

Look at that, one thing settled for our wedding. Now, if we could pick a date and get the invites sent out, it would be a miracle. Still, I don't pester her about it. She has a vision of what her perfect day will look like, and unfortunately, my job and her potential job, are clouding that for her. I wish I could help her, ease her mind on these trivial things, but I can't. She's right. The industry of professionals we surround ourselves with will not understand why she's getting married in the winter. Wives and girlfriends know better, according to the old-timers. Some still believe that weddings and babies only happen in the offseason. I don't necessarily disagree, except my girl wants to be married at Christmas, even if she won't come out and say it.

"Do you know who you're picking as your best man?"

I shake my head. "It's either my dad or Quinn."

"Not Nick?" she asks.

Again, I tell her no silently. As close as I am with Nick, asking him would hurt my dad's feelings, and that's not something I am comfortable doing. My dad would tell me that he understands, but deep down I know he won't. He's still, to this day, trying to make up for those ten years we lost.

"I think both would be honored."

"What about you, have you asked Elle?"

Peyton smiles softly. "Not yet, she's so busy with her job and trying to build a band that I haven't wanted to broach the subject with her. What if she says no?"

I lean forward and cup her cheek. My thumb moves back and forth against her soft skin. "Sometimes I wonder what goes on in your head. This is your sister we're talking about. Not just any sister, but your *twin*. You know better than anyone that she's expecting you to ask her and you also know she'll drop everything to be by your side."

"But is it fair, to ask her I mean? She's trying to build a career."

What a loaded question. As far as I'm concerned, we're all trying to build our careers. My showing as a quarterback hasn't been stellar by any means. Peyton, with offers from major networks, must decide on what she plans to do. Elle is a budding music manager. And Quinn, I think he's the only one who's content doing his own thing.

"And so are you, but this is your wedding, your sister will be by your side. I think you know this, but are trying to find excuses as to why we shouldn't get married this year."

Her mouth drops open. A good boyfriend, fiancé, and partner would backtrack his comment. While I am good, I'm not taking back what I said. I've gotten the feeling from her for a while that the timing is off, and maybe it is, but she needs to know that we don't have to get married this year or even next. I'm not going anywhere.

I pick up her left hand and kiss the ring I placed on

her finger. "I love you, Peyton, with everything that I am, but I get the feeling you're not ready to get married."

"I am, Noah."

"But?"

She takes her hand away and covers her face. The shudder of her shoulders has me pulling her into my arms as much as I can. I'm an idiot for bringing this up on the plane, of all places, where people could hear what we're saying. "I'm sorry," I whisper into her ear.

"Don't be. You're right to question me. Lately, I've felt... off. I can't explain it."

"We can wait, Peyton."

She pulls away and shakes her head as she wipes a few tears from her cheeks. "I don't want to wait, I want things to make sense."

"What's not making sense?"

"Me. Life. Us. I shouldn't be here, Noah. I should've died in that car accident and yet, I'm alive and well, and I feel like something is missing or I'm supposed to do something astonishing as some kind of payback for surviving."

I can't compete with her inner demons. She's been battling them for some time now, and no amount of therapy or group support has helped. None of us understand what she's going through or what she's been through for that matter, no matter how hard we try. We may have sat by her bedside, praying, hoping, and wishing she'd wake-up, all the while she was having an out of body experience, and more and more of those memories are haunting her.

The flight attendant announces that we'll be landing soon. I help Peyton gather her magazines and slip them back into the bag. We hold hands, but she stares out the window for the remainder of our flight, all while panic bubbles deep within me. I can't lose her. That happened once, and I wanted to give up. But if I can't save her, I don't know what I'm going to do.

Being back home in Portland means fans recognize you. Peyton is a saint, standing there while I take pictures and sign autographs. The best part though, is that the fans congratulate us, even though our engagement is old news. They're eager to see pictures of her dress, the flowers, and asks if we're selling our photos to People magazine.

Honestly, neither of us have given much thought to their offer. Nor has Peyton decided whether she will go on Say Yes To The Dress. Elle wants her to, but Peyton and her sister are vastly different from each other. Where one is flashy and in your face, the other is reserved and prefers to stand back in the crowd.

By the time we reach the luggage carousel, the driver with the car service I hired already has our bags. Our boxes and furniture will arrive in about two weeks, most of it will go to storage until we decide what we're going to do, either buy a house or a condominium. Everything in my apartment is staying there, which is good. I have a tough time separating the fact that Dessie used to be in the apartment and now Peyton is. She's never said anything, but sometimes I can sense a bit of uneasiness from her.

The drive downtown is done in silence. Peyton stares out of the window and I've found a new fascination with the threading on my jeans. The tension in the car is thick, and it troubles me. I reach for her hand, and it comes freely. She links her fingers with mine and squeezes. It's her way of telling me that everything is okay.

I worry about her leaving me. Not every day, but when she's like this, it's all I can think about. I have to stop and think, put myself in her shoes, when her mind starts wandering into the dark. She can't help it. She's tried. And most of the time it's triggered by an event she's seen on television or read about in the paper. Or when someone asks her about her scars.

When we finally pull up to the valet, I get out and rush to her side. I open her door, take her hand in mine, and scoop her up into my arms, twirling her around. She squeals and it's the happiest fucking sound in the world to me right now.

"We're home, at least temporarily," I say to her as she slides down my torso. Her hands rest on my cheeks and she looks into my eyes.

"I don't deserve you."

"You do," I remind her. "We were destined to be together, to walk through life as one."

She rises on her toes and kisses me. "I can't wait to be your wife."

I let her words linger between us, hoping she hears herself for a minute before I drop down onto my knee. She looks at me oddly, and then at the people who are coming in and out of the hotel where our apartment is located. They gasp, but my Peyton is utterly confused.

"Peyton, will you marry me?" I ask, reaching for her hand. There are a few ahs coming from the onlookers and one yells, "If you won't, I will."

"Noah, what are you doing?"

"I don't know, but it feels right to ask you again as we start this next chapter of our lives. You've given up Chicago for me, and I just have to make sure you know how much I love you."

"I do know, now stand up, people are staring." She laughs as she tugs on my shoulder, helping me stand.

"Excuse me," I holler to the people lingering. "This woman has agreed to be my wife, to put up with my whining, complaining, and the bellyaching I do after practice. She's my best friend, my cheerleader and the mother of my future children, but most importantly, my partner!" I turn to Peyton, who looks completely stunned. "Whatever you need, Peyton, I'll give it to you." I lean down and kiss her, much to the delight of the people around us.

When we part, she socks me in the gut. "You're a pain in my butt," she seethes.

"I know." I gasp for air. "But you're smiling, so it's worth it."

The elevator ride results in Peyton rubbing the spot where she punched me. I may be over exaggerating my pain a little bit, but it's worth it. I'm going to milk it for as long as I can. At our apartment, I unlock the door and let her enter before me. She gasps, and I smile, knowing full well what she's walked in to. I shut the door quietly and come behind, wrapping my arms around her.

"Welcome home."

The company I hired to decorate the inside of the apartment went above and beyond my expectations. The large 'welcome to our home' sign is eye-catching and beautiful, and something that will hang in our next home. Flowers fill the room. Roses, peonies, daisies, and hydrangeas cover every open surface. But it's the bottle of champagne and the tray of strawberries that catches my attention.

"What do you think, future Mrs. Westbury, should we drink that bottle in the tub?"

"I'll start the water, you grab the goods." She turns in my arms. "I'll meet you there."

I lean down to kiss her but she's off and moving rather

15

quickly down the hall, all while leaving a trail of clothes for me to follow. Right now, I'm not going to pay attention to her sudden mood change. I'll chalk it up to traveling or whatnot, but I am going to pay attention. If planning our wedding is causing her to retreat, maybe it's time we rethink our plans.

3

PEYTON

*M*inus the heat and humidity, Chicago and Portland aren't all that different. They're both bustling, overcrowded metropolises. However, I love it here and one of my favorite things to do is go to the Saturday market along the waterfront. I've been able to buy so many amazing trinkets for our home, as well as fresh vegetables, fruit, and the most beautiful bouquets. Noah doesn't always come down with me, which gives me an opportunity to really explore. He's too well known, and people don't hesitate to ask him for his autograph or to pose for a picture. Even if he wears a disguise, someone always figures it out. You would think, that after growing up with the band, I would be used to it. In some ways, I am. I expect the fans to recognize Noah, my dad, Liam, and Jimmy, but I don't always like it.

This morning, I'm sitting in Pioneer Courthouse Square with a cup of coffee in my hand, watching as people rush to work. They come and go in droves, getting off the train and buses before disappearing into the skyscrapers surrounding me. The bricks that make up the square contain names of the community members who help bring the project to life. The names below my feet, the ones I'm sitting on and the ones that surround me, make me wonder what their life was like, who they were and what they've become since the early 80s.

The bell from the nearby church rings out. I count each one, it's nine and time for my dilly-dallying to end. If others have things to do, they're not hurrying off. They're lingering, enjoying the sun, and reveling in the beauty that is all around them. I want to stay, and probably would if there weren't more pressing issues weighing on my mind.

A few blocks down, where the older buildings are, I push a heavy steel door open and climb a flight of narrow stairs. Inside, the room is warm, the sun beating through the windows. A few people look at me as I enter. I smile softly and choose one of the seats in the back. The advantage of sitting there is the fact that I'm close to the door and can make a quick escape if I feel like I can't manage the meeting well. The disadvantage is that when I go to speak, everyone will turn and look at me. They do it out of respect, so they can hear your words and let them soak in.

"Good morning." His name is Barry, he's a grief counselor, and comes highly recommended. He sits on a stool, wearing corduroy pants and a tweed blazer. Very outdated, but very Portland. "I want to thank each of you for coming today. I know that sometimes you struggle with waking up, so the fact that you not only woke up but also got dressed and made your way here, speaks volumes about how your day is going to go. Would anyone care to start?"

Someone in front raises their hands. I careen my neck to see, but the people in front of me are taller, making me wish I had chosen a better seat.

"Last week, I lost my husband." Her voice is soft, and I almost couldn't hear her, but I did, and her words stab me in the heart. Noah... he's always on my mind. My constant everything. I desperately want to be his wife, but fear he will be ostracized by his teammates, his coach, and the media. Players "know better" than to get married during the season or have children. Wives have been the butt end of jokes when they give birth between August and the end of January, saying we know better. And I do. I know that football is an old boys club, that it's hard for women to break through the mold. I also know that I'm going to be damn good at whatever my job turns out being, but being Noah's wife is also important to me. Maybe more so than a job.

"Twenty years, and he's gone," she concludes. I'm so lost in my head that I didn't hear what else she had to say.

"I'm sorry for your loss," Barry says, and everyone else repeats him. "Anyone else?"

I raise my hand. I don't know why, but I do. These people are strangers, and yet here I am, about to share my story with them. It's cathartic. I tried once to get Kyle to come with me in Chicago, so he could understand why there are times when I need to distance myself from him, but he couldn't or wouldn't. I don't remember the excuse.

"I'm Peyton," I tell the group of about fifteen. "I died." I let the heaviness of my word settle over the group. There are a few gasps, and of course, there's always the one or two who don't believe me. My mom is part of the latter or part of the 'nonbelievers' where she doesn't want to believe her daughter died and came back. I'm not sure which is better, to be honest. "I was in a horrific accident a few winters ago. The car I was a passenger in was t-boned by a semi. The irony is that my father died after a similar accident." I readjust the way I'm sitting and look at the back of the grayish brown metal chair, focusing on the little gold label. "Like I said, I died and came back, but haven't felt right since."

"Like a piece is missing?"

I look to my right. The woman at the end of the row is bent at her waist and looking at me. I smile and nod. "Yes, like something was left on the other side."

"I feel the same way," she mumbles.

"Peyton," Barry says my name to get my attention. "I want to welcome you to the group and thank you for being here."

"Thank you," everyone says in unison.

"Death and dying are part of the unknown. If we could quantify what people experience, both good and bad, I believe we'd have an upheaval on our hands. Meaning people would experiment more to have the experiences of others, which is not necessarily a good thing."

"It wasn't fun," I tell him. Except for seeing my father and knowing how badly I wanted to go with him. I've missed him growing up, but since my accident, he's all I think about. I keep this tidbit to myself. Not even Noah knows because I don't want him to think I'm going to do something to myself. I don't want him to worry. "I was in a lot of pain. I've had a lot of surgeries, and the scars I bear remind me every day of how close I came to losing my life forever."

"Three years ago, I lost my son to a drive-by." My story is interrupted. I'm both grateful and slightly annoyed. What if I wasn't finished? What if I had more to tell? What if... what if I wanted sympathy, for someone to tell me that everything is going to be okay, that it'll all work out if I just... that's just it, no one knows. Least of all me.

By the time the session is over, I've zoned out. The woman on the end, the one who knows what I'm going through is at the coffee station. I go there, with the intent to speak to her, but I can't find the words. We stand side-by-side, stirring powdered creamer into our coffee with a wooden stick. I pick mine up and make eye contact with her. I smile and head for the door.

"Wait up," I hear as soon as I hit the street. There are horns honking, people yelling and freight trucks making all sorts of racket, but I hear her. She walks toward me with coffee sloshing out of her cup. "I'm Frankie."

"Peyton," I say as we shake hands.

"Are you in a rush to get to work?"

"No," I tell her. "I was just going to walk back to the square and sit before I go home. Sometimes after group, I need time to decompress."

"Same, do you mind if I walk with you?"

I shake my head and start in the direction we need to go. Our bodies jostle with people rushing by us, making me wish I had a lid for my coffee. When we come to a food cart, I stop and order us two fresh cups. "Thanks," she says.

We sit down, and I lift my face to the sun. As much as I love the summer, I love football and that means fall. I'm counting down the days until Noah starts practice. I want to be there, on the sidelines, for every game, which is another reason why I shouldn't go to work. Noah tells me to make my own choice, to follow my path and not his. It's been his family's motto since he was reunited with his dad. *Follow only your dreams*. Noah will support me in whatever I decide. I know this. What I don't know is, what my path is.

"I have cystic fibrosis," Frankie says after a few minutes. "About two years ago, I got really sick. My parents had last rites done, funeral was planned, and somehow, I woke up. And, I didn't want to."

"Me neither," I tell her. "I was five when my father died. He was there, waiting for me. All I had to do was take his hand."

"And there would be no more pain."

I nod. "But then I wouldn't be here and right now I'm where I always dreamed of being."

"Sitting on brick steps drinking coffee from a food truck?" She lifts her cup and laughs.

"No, engaged to the only man I've ever loved. Surrounded by an amazing family."

"But they don't understand," she adds, and I agree with her. "I do, so if you ever want to talk, I'm here."

"Me too," I say. We sit for a few minutes, staring off. The both of us lost in our own thoughts. "Are you sick now?"

She shrugs. "I'm always on meds. I know when my lung function is dropping so I'll check myself into the hospital. Usually stay about a week or two, depending on how fast I can kick the infection. There are new advances in medicine, helping prolong our lives, but they don't work for everyone."

"That's too bad. Do you have a good support group?"

She shakes her head. "CFers aren't supposed to hang out with each other because we can share bacteria. We cough a lot and covering our mouths doesn't always work when another patient is around, so we try to keep our distance."

"So, you really are alone?" She nods. "Wow, I'm sorry."

"I'm used to it. The isolation that is. My parents, they try but their concern is my health and I hear, 'did you take your meds' way too many times a day. It would be nice if they just asked how my day was."

"How's your day, Frankie?" I ask.

She smiles. "So far, it's been pretty good. Yours?"

"No complaints here."

"What do you do for work, Peyton?"

"Nothing, yet. I recently graduated from Northwestern."

"And you moved here?"

"My fiancé lives here, his job is here, it made sense to be here. Chicago was nice, it's a lot like Portland in ways."

"We have Voodoo Donuts," she points out.

"Yes, there's definitely that."

Frankie and I chat for another hour or so before I tell her I need to head home. It was nice to speak to someone about life, even if Frankie is in a different place in life. Knowing someone understands how unsettled I feel sometimes helps.

Back at the apartment, I say hi to the bellhop as he holds the door for me and listen to the couple on the elevator talk animatedly about how excited they are to visit the City of Roses. In our apartment, music blares from one of the spare rooms. I don't bother knocking on the door, and just open it because I know the sight behind it is better than making Noah stop, and I'm right. My soon-to-be-husband is shirtless and lifting weights. He installed a set of mirrors when he made himself a home gym and from where I stand, I can see the concentration on his face. And a smile, which is meant just for me.

4

NOAH

*T*he smell of freshly baked cookies washes over me as soon as Peyton and I step inside my parents' home. My stomach growls loudly as Betty Paige's eyes light up as soon as she sees me and she comes thundering down the steps and into my arms. I don't care how many times a month I see her, each time I can't believe how much she's grown. I don't want to think about her dating, wearing makeup or even looking at colleges. She may have arrived when I was almost a teenager, but I wanted her.

"Can you please stop growing?"

"Daddy says the same thing each time I go shopping," she laughs.

"That's because you max out my credit card." My dad comes into the room. We hug briefly before he pulls Peyton into his arms. I watch their exchange. It's fatherly, with her hanging on for dear life. "We're glad to have you both home," he says after letting the love of my life go. Reaching for Peyton's hand, I pull her close and kiss her forehead.

"Where's Mom?" Peyton and I decided to come home to Beaumont so she and my mom can get a head start on flowers. No date, but we'll have flowers.

"At the shop. She's getting some samples ready for you guys to look at," Paige says. "We can go over them now, that's if you want my help." She shrugs and looks at Peyton. I know she's fishing for a spot in the wedding party and have no doubt Peyton will ask her.

"Of course, I'd love your opinion," Peyton tells her. Try as she might, Betty Paige's face lights up. Being a part of the wedding is her dream. She texts me with ideas all the time, asking if I think Peyton will like this or that.

"How was the flight?" My dad picks Peyton's bag up and heads toward the stairwell. I follow, but Peyton stays with my sister.

"Perfect. It's so nice to just relax." I'm spoiled, but so are Peyton, Quinn, Elle, Betty Paige, and Eden. When it's convenient, we can use the private jet. It's a luxury that I wish I could use when the team flies. Not many people realize how big a nose tackle is or an offensive lineman. Big, beefy, most are tall and just overly large men. Try sitting next to one of them on a plane. It doesn't bode well for any of us.

"And Peyton, how's she doing with the move?" he asks, setting her bag down on the bed in what used to be my room. It's no longer the "boy" room it once was, although my trophies are still here but now they're nice and tidy on a shelf. This room has become a guest room and my mom likes to tease my dad that it will be a nursery in a few years once grandbabies start to arrive. Ever see a grown man quiver? Mention grandchildren and watch my dad and Harrison shake at the knees. It's comical.

"She's doing really well. She likes her new therapist and has a friend from her support group who has been through a similar situation."

"I worry about her. We all do."

"She's good," I tell him. "I take care of her." And I do. I won't let anything happen to her.

"Noah?" she calls for me from downstairs. I wonder if there will ever be a time when hearing her say my name won't cause a stirring. I duck my head and discreetly adjust my pants. My dad laughs and slaps me on my shoulder.

"I feel the same when it comes to your mom."

Gross. Gag. Barf. No, just no. I can't. I refuse to think of my parents doing... not gonna happen. "Right, I'm going to go bleach my ears now." This only makes my dad laugh harder.

"He's coming, Peyton." Again, with another snicker.

My cheeks are instantly on fire. I can't believe my dad, who somehow thinks my embarrassment is funny. I give myself a few moments, taking in some deep breaths to calm myself down before I head to the stairs. My breathing hitches as I see her, the woman who I'm hoping will be my wife by the end of the year, standing there looking up at me. Her dark hair is plaited and hanging over her shoulder. Her blue eyes, growing more expectant as I take each step toward her.

When I finally reach her, I lean down and kiss her softly. "I love you," I tell her. I say these words a lot, multiple times a day because I don't want her to forget. Not that I think she would, but I think it's important that she knows at random times throughout her day. The words shouldn't be reserved for when we're parting or after making love, but for when she's standing in the kitchen or when she's come in from a run.

"I love you too. Are you ready?"

I nod just as my dad comes back into the room. "Peyton are you okay if I steal your groom away for a bit?"

"Dad, we are about to look at flowers."

"You can have him," she says. I look at her and she winks. "Between your mom and sister, I think I'll be able to come up with a good idea. Besides, it's not like we can't show you later. We do know the owner," she laughs, and I'm trying to figure out if she's really okay going by herself. My dad hands her the keys to his car, and she waves as her and Paige head out.

"What just happened?"

"She's giving you a reprieve."

"I get that, but I want to go with her."

My dad pats me on the back. "Give her some time with your mom. You can check in with her later and if you feel like you need to be there, we can go over. There's something I want to show you."

As much as I don't want to agree with my dad, he's right. He did warn me that some of the wedding planning will be done by the moms and sisters, and I just have to sit back and wait. Thing is, I want Peyton to know that I care, that it's not just a day where I'll show up. I want to be present in the process, right alongside her. And right now is the time, because once training starts, my time is limited.

Still, I follow my dad to his truck, even though I'd rather be with Peyton. Once we're on the road, the drive becomes familiar and I find myself looking in the back for a cooler of beer. Sure enough, the old faded red ice box is back there. Question is, is it full?

We pull into the field where generations of parties have happened, except something's changed. For one, the tower has been painted red and Beaumont stands out in white. However, that's not what stands out the most. There's a staircase leading to the top. I get out of the truck and stare dumbfounded at it.

"What the fu—"

"My thoughts exactly," my dad says appearing next to me with the cooler in his hand. "Some kid fell last year and broke his leg. His parents tried to sue the city, so the council tried to remove the ladder altogether. A bunch of guys that I went to school with, who have kids, fought back. Saying the city was taking away a piece of our heritage. This is the answer."

"A staircase so anyone can climb up."

"Yep." He nods toward the tower. I look over to find two figures waving back. "Nick and Mack are up there."

"No shit?" My dad and Nick aren't exactly friends, but not enemies either. I think it's pretty stand-up of my dad to put his feelings aside so I can have a relationship with Nick.

"Come on, we have guy stuff to talk about."

I follow my dad up the stairs. It's nice that I'm not worrying about my life, but they defeat the purpose of having to climb a ladder to get up there. Still, the view is amazing once we're at the top.

Mack rushes over to me and shakes my hand. I squeeze it a bit tighter than I should, sending him a message that despite the relationship I have with his dad, I am Paige's big brother and she will always come first. There's no secret that they have crushes on each other and I know both parents have gone to extremes to keep a tight eye on them.

Nick follows, but he and I hug. We're as close as father and son. "Good to see you."

"You too," he says. Because of his coaching schedule, he doesn't get to Portland often to see me play. He'll make one game this upcoming season, two if he gets bounced from the playoffs, but from what my dad and Nick have been saying, Beaumont High is going to be a powerhouse this year. They have a running back similar to my uncle Mason.

"So, I feel like this is some sort of intervention," I say as I sit down. My dad hands me a beer, one to Nick and a soda for Mack.

"Nah, just some dad time," Nick adds. Beside me, my dad cringes and I laugh. Some things will never change.

"Noah, are you ready for the season?" Mack asks.

I shrug. "I will be. Right now, I'm still in vacation mode."

"Yeah, me too," Mack replies. I look down the row at him. He's drinking the can of soda, almost as if he's an adult sucking down a beer.

"Aren't you still in school? In season?"

Nick sighs. "He is, but he's on this teenage kick of growing up faster than he needs to."

"Keep him away from Betty Paige," my dad mumbles. I second that notion. I remember puberty all too well and there was only one thing I cared about, aside from sports, and that was the attention I got from girls.

"Your dad and I thought we'd plan your bachelor party."

"Quinn isn't here," I point out to Nick. "I'd like him to be involved."

"Is he your best man?" Mack asks.

I nod, realizing at this moment that I want Quinn to

stand next to me. "I'm going to ask him when we go camping. I figured that'll be a good time. I just hope he says yes."

"Why wouldn't he?" Dad asks.

I look at him, wondering if he wanted to be my best man. "Quinn's not really a flashy guy and being a best man puts him on display. He'll have to give a speech."

Nick and my dad laugh. "I think there will be plenty of speeches at your wedding."

"When is it?" Mack asks.

Going silent, I shrug. "Peyton and I are still working out the details. I'm hoping soon."

"Do you know where at least?" Nick wants to know.

"Here, definitely in Beaumont. She wants to be close to her father and where we grew up. Says this is our home and where we should get married."

The dads seem to be in agreement, which is always nice. All the wedding talk though has me itching to get a date set, and I'm hoping after meeting with my mom, Peyton finally opens the calendar and puts her finger on a date. I don't care when, I'll be there.

As soon as I finish my beer, I toss it down to the bed of Nick's truck. I don't know why, but the sound of breaking glass is very satisfying. At least, I thought so until Mack speaks.

"I can't wait until I can drink beer."

Nick's mouthful of ale sprays out of his mouth. My dad laughs, until he starts choking. "Mack, you have a long way until you're of age."

"How old were you when you had your first one?"

I look at Nick, who knows the answer won't be good if I say something. "Drinking isn't cool, Mack. You should focus on school and sports."

"And girls," he says. "Well, at least one."

I bite my tongue. I remember what it was like, being his age, but this boy has a set of cajones on him like no other, saying this stuff in front of my dad. I'm just glad I'm not in his shoes.

5

PEYTON

The flowers I picked up at the local market smell amazing. Across the way, there's a funeral going on. I wish I could remember the day we buried my father. Was it raining? Did we sing? Did my mom cry? In my mind, I think I know what went on, but I can't be certain. I do know that Liam sat next to me and held my hand. He became the man I could count on until my dad took over that role. Still, with Liam poised to be my father-in-law, I couldn't have asked for a better man.

I clear away grass clippings from my father's tombstone. My fingers instantly go back to his name, tracing the letters. The memories I have of him from when I was little, have all faded. It's the memories from a few years ago that haunt me. I see my father when I sleep. He invades my dreams. He's there when I'm staring out a window lost in thought or sitting in the oversized chair that I love so much. Whenever I find myself daydreaming, he's there.

Thankfully, I can say he's not floating in and out of

my walls or trying to scare me at night. Still, I can't explain what he is, a ghost, spirit, a figment conjured up in my mind. He's just there. I can feel him, see him sitting on the couch. Sometimes I sense him when Noah's home, when we're together watching television. I can hear his laughter.

Telling Noah would be the smart thing to do but finding the words to admit that you're seeing things is really hard. My therapist suggested I go to hypnotherapy, and I've even considered a medium. Neither sound like a pleasant option if I'm honest. I'm not positive that I want to reach my father because I'm afraid he'll ask me to join him on the other side or tell me not to marry Noah, and I don't know if I'm strong enough to tell him no.

After I have the bouquet arranged in the cemetery provided vase, I sit and rest my back against the slab of granite. Elle and I had this placed years ago, replacing the existing marker. The original held a space for our mom, but neither of us would bring her here to be buried with our father. She belongs, when the time comes, with our dad and wherever they end up.

"There are times when I wish you were here, although I don't know how our lives would be. Mom, Elle, and I love Harrison, and can't imagine him not being a part of our lives. I'm grateful for him because he stepped in when he didn't have to. He was there when I needed someone and has always looked at me like a daughter. Then I think you would've done the same thing in the same situation, but it's hard to picture you there, because I can only remember Harrison being there. Sometimes I feel like I've failed as your daughter. Grandpa says I haven't, that only a heart truly remembers a love and that eyes forget.

"And that's what I'm trying to do now, Dad. Forget. I want to forget the accident, the surgeries, the pain I was in. I don't want to flinch when Noah touches me or wonder if I'm going to sit down and find you next to me. I don't know, maybe my therapist is right, and I need to see someone who can help me explore my memories because I think you're stuck on this side and can't get back. Have you been here this whole time?"

Of course, there's no one to answer me. Right now, would be an ideal time for my dad to appear, take form in another person and come over here, but no, I'm here alone, aside from the funeral taking place right now. I don't want to stare, but I'm curious. Beaumont is a small town, everyone knows everyone, yet somehow, I don't know who has passed away. Last year, when Elle and I lost a classmate, our phones were ringing off the hook. His death rocked our little community, and while we couldn't make it to his service, Josie represented our families. I never asked her about the service or even checked in with her. Maybe that's why I haven't heard about this one going on today, she probably thinks I don't care.

I do. I care deeply.

Thoughts of Josie spur me to take my phone out. I flip through the pictures I took yesterday of the arrangements she made for me. Every one of them had Paige oohing and awing, proclaiming it was her favorite until her mom brought out another one. I have my favorite though.

There's no denying that I want a winter wedding. I've imagined the red and white roses from the day Noah asked me to marry him. His parents were married after Christmas, and mine, well they made us a family on the same night, professing their love for each other. I want to honor them both. Doing so, means taking criticism from the people we surround ourselves with on a daily basis, and I don't know if I can do that to Noah.

The last bouquet sealed my desire to marry Noah in December though. The soft pinks, whites and dark reds mixed together created something I had never dreamed of. The spirea, peonies, Japanese lisianthus, scabiosa, sweet peas, roses, anemones, hellebores, and olive and bay branches cascading down brought a tear to my eye. Josie knew too, she nodded and said this is the one. It was. It is. It's what I want. I held it in front of me and looked into the mirror. Paige and Josie stood on either side.

"Just imagine your mom and sister here, dressed in cream and red. Noah and his party, dressed in gray suits."

I turn and look at her. "Did Noah tell you this?"

She shakes her head.

How did she know that's what I wanted? Noah and I barely discussed what he could potentially wear, and yet his mother had the same vision.

I wipe away a fallen tear, wondering if it's from happiness or the unsurmountable anxiety I feel by sitting here. The committal service is over, the family and friends of whoever lies in the coffin leaving them there for a caretaker to put into the ground. How morbid, I think. And how lonely the person inside the coffin must feel.

Turning my attention back to my dad, I brush my fingers over his name once again. "I think, had I not been in the accident, I wouldn't have to ask you this question, but I need to know if you can leave me alone. I'm trying to build a life with Noah and he worries about me. I think he's afraid I'm going to do something to hurt myself so I can go back to where I was with you, and I don't want him to stress. I love him and want to be with him. I love you too, but I need for you to let me be, let me move on. I love you, Daddy." I kiss my hand and place it on top of the tombstone before walking away.

I'm almost to my car when my phone rings. I expect it to be Noah, but the number is unfamiliar. "Hello?"

"Peyton James?"

"Yes, who's calling?"

"This is Leo Bowen from the Rams. Have I caught you at a bad time?"

"Uh, no. What can I do for you?"

"We'd like to invite you out to our offices in Los Angeles. We know you have offers from ESPN, Fox, and the NFL Network, and believe you haven't accepted a job as of yet, is this correct?"

"Yes, it is."

"Perfect. We're interested in you."

"To do what exactly?"

"Player analysis. We like the way you break down the game, point out the weaknesses, the abilities and pinpoint where the players and coaching staff need to make adjustments."

My mind goes crazy at the thought of working in player development. It wasn't a path I thought I wanted to pursue, not until I helped Noah fix the issue with his feet. I clear my throat. "Are you offering me a job?"

"We are, if you're interested."

"I... I don't know. I think I am but would need some time." Time for what, Peyton? Aside from discussing this with Noah, who will tell me to do what I want, what will time do?

"Are you interested in at least coming out here, seeing the facilities and meeting the staff?"

"I am," I tell him with a smile on my face. "Very much so."

"That's great. I'm going to put you on with my secretary to help make the arrangements." Ten minutes later I'm speeding home to tell Noah. When I get back to the Westbury's, I run into the house, yelling his name.

Noah comes running around the corner and reaches for my arms. "What's wrong? Are you hurt?"

I shake my head and smile. "I was offered a job." I hold up my phone as if he can hear the conversation I had earlier.

"Like three of them," he points out, but I'm shaking my head so fast it's starting to hurt.

"No," I wheeze, almost out of breath. "The Rams just called and offered me a job in player development, doing game and player breakdowns."

Noah's eyes go wide. He picks me up and spins me around. Just like he did with the other job offers. Once I'm back on my feet, he kisses me deeply. "I'm so proud of you."

"I haven't done anything yet," I remind him. "They want me to come to LA."

"Go!"

I laugh. "I am, tomorrow."

His face falls, but the smile remains. I'm interrupting the rest of our week together and next week he'll be with my dad and brother, which means I won't see him for days. "I can reschedule."

"Absolutely not. You'll go and knock their socks off. Wow, babe. I'm so happy for you." We kiss until we hear his dad clearing his throat. I retell my story and Liam suggests we go out to dinner to celebrate.

At the restaurant, we're out in the open. This doesn't

happen for us in Portland or even Los Angeles, but here in Beaumont, no one cares that Liam Page is stuffing his face with a giant burger or that Noah Westbury can't take his eyes off me.

Betty Paige recounts her day in school, telling us that there's a new girl in town and she already has eyes for Mack.

"You should let him date her," Liam says, which causes Paige to cry. Her and Mack are star-crossed lovers, the Romeo and Juliet of town. Their fathers' history plays a huge role in their love life, not that they should have one at this age, but it does. Liam refuses to let her date at all, let alone date Nick's son.

"Daddy, how can you say such a thing?"

"You're not old enough to date, Paige. That's how."

"But I love him." She throws her hands up in the air and collapses into her mother, who tries to console her. At this age, I kept my crush a secret. Probably for the same reasons. No one would ever let Noah and I date, not with five years between us.

"Paige," I say her name to get her attention. "Trust me when I say this, love will wait." Noah squeezes my hand under the table.

"How can you be so sure?"

"Because it waited for me."

Noah leans over and whispers, "I'd wait forever if you needed me to."

I duck my head and smile. I won't need him to wait. Once this job interview is done, I'm going to pick a date and marry the man of my dreams. I look back at Paige. "And I wanted to ask if you'd do me the honor of being one of my bridesmaids?"

She stands and comes rushing over, wrapping her

arms around me. "Yes, yes, yes! Thank you so much, Peyton."

"You're welcome, sweetie, and thank you."

One decision down, many to go. I'm not sure if I can plan a wedding in six months, but I'm going to try.

6

NOAH

*C*amping deep in the woods of Mt. Hood, was my dad's idea. He set this trip up months ago, and the timing of it couldn't be more perfect. With Peyton in Los Angeles, I'm a nervous wreck. If this trip hadn't been planned, I would be there with her right now.

After stepping into the clearing, I pause and take a deep breath. The crisp mountain air of Oregon is one of my favorite things about living here. Within an hour I can be at the beach. Head the other direction and I'm in the mountains.

The first time I brought my dad out here, we sat for hours on a boulder, watching the water rush over the rocks like a battering ram. The sheer force that the run-off creates, coming off the mountain, is a remarkable sight. Each time he visits, in the offseason, I take him somewhere new. It's my way of filling the void I feel when it comes to him.

Our campsite is isolated from the road, but not other campers. On each side of us, tents are set up, with fires burning in the cylinder pits, and the smell of campfire wafts through the air. The only drawback to camping is that my clothes will smell, and after a while, it can be bothersome.

Harrison pulls out a collapsible broom, extending the handle until it's full height. "What are you doing?" Quinn asks before I can get the words to come out. Harrison looks confused by his son's question.

"Sweeping the ground."

Sweeping the ground? Does he not realize that we're under pine and evergreen trees and that anything he clears away now will only resurface later? We're in the middle of the forest. Surely, he understands this.

Quinn runs his hand over his beanie and looks at me. I shrug. I can't help him where his father's cleanliness habits are concerned. I can see the wheels turning in Quinn's mind. He looks back at his dad and asks, "Um, why?"

I want to laugh, but I don't. Truth is, I'm tempted to know the answer as well.

"So the ground is clean."

"Aren't the pine needles supposed to give us a barrier, maybe some kind of comfort?"

Quinn has a point, but I stay silent as Harrison stops and looks at all of us. After a long beat, Harrison throws his hands up in the air, the broom goes flying, and loudly proclaims, "I don't know. I'm only doing what Katelyn suggested."

We laugh. All three of us. Harrison looks a bit put off. He waves us off and retrieves his broom and puts it back in his bag.

Did you ever hear the joke about the three musicians and the quarterback who went camping deep into the woods without any cell reception? No? Me neither, but

I'm hoping these few days don't turn out to be a nightmare.

"Let's get our tent set up." I tap Quinn on the arm who's still watching his dad's every move. There's definitely a bit of tension between them. It's not something I've ever sensed before, which is probably why it's noticeable. Quinn's the quiet type though, otherwise, I'd totally ask him what's going on. I just know that if I wait, he'll tell me when he's ready.

Together, we work to get our tent laid out, making sure that when we wake up, we're looking at the river and not our fathers. The dads follow suit, and once we're done, we string a couple of tarps up to help keep us dry in the event of rain.

Watching Quinn, I realize that I'm definitely going to ask him to be my best man. When I first met him, I hated him, for no other reason than he got to spend his life with my dad. My dad was there when he came to live with Harrison as a baby, there for all of Quinn's birthdays, holidays, and everything else in between. They have childhood memories together, and I was jealous. Still am to this day, even though I've long gotten over the hatred I've felt. There are times when I want to ask Quinn what my dad was like back then, but deep down I don't want to know. I don't want to hear about women, drugs, drinking, or any of those things because I only truly know my dad when he's been with my mom. The image I have of my father is one that I don't want to change, and I fear if Quinn and I delve into the past, it could alter my view of my dad. So, I stay quiet and leave my thoughts in my head because, in the end, Quinn has been nothing but a brother to me, even when I didn't deserve his friendship.

I know we left our fishing poles in the car and motion

for Quinn to follow me. I'm not looking forward to hiking two miles back to the car, but it'll give us some privacy. Not only am I asking him to stand next to me, but I'm asking him to do it while I'm marrying his sister. When you think about it, we're that cliché of the best friend falling for the sister, and I've never once considered his feelings on the matter. Not that I can change what's happening now. I'm going to marry Peyton, no matter what.

"What'd you forget?" he asks, halfway up the path.

"Just going to grab the fishing poles," I tell him. I can't recall a time he and I have ever fished together, not that we would've. Camping isn't exactly a thing in our families. Give us the beach, surfboards and we're happy, especially if we're all together.

The whole way to the car and back to the campsite, I chicken out asking Quinn the all-important question. I swear, asking Peyton to marry me, was much easier. Still, by the time we get back, I haven't been able to find the words and I'm kicking myself.

Our dads have started a fire, cracked open a few beers and look completely relaxed, which is the whole point of this trip.

"You kids hungry?" my dad asks as soon as Quinn and I put our gear down.

"We're not kids anymore, Dad," I point out. I search through the cooler and toss a pre-made sandwich to Quinn. I made my dad stop at this corner deli that I love so much and stock up on their fresh bread, pickles, lunch-meat, and cheese. I also ordered us a few sandwiches to get us started with. I hand Quinn a soda. I probably should've asked if he wanted a beer, but I selfishly didn't because I can't have one. I only have a few weeks before training starts and I want to be in the best shape possible when I take the field.

"So, what's the plan for these four days?" Quinn asks.

"Absolutely nothing," Harrison says. "We're here to rest, relax, recoup, and reenergize." Harrison stares hard at Quinn, which to me only drives home the fact that I think there's something amiss between the two of them, and really making me wish Peyton was here so I could ask her.

I sit down next to Quinn and start to inhale my sandwich. I've gotten into the habit of eating fast when I'm around other guys. I don't know if it's because I'm always in a rush to go watch game film or head back to the practice field or if I'm worried that one of my linemen is going to steal my food.

The sharp jab that Quinn gives my ribs pulls me away from the sub I'm trying to devour in no time flat. "Dude, this isn't jail. You don't have five minutes to eat."

I swallow what's in my mouth and laugh. "How would you know what jail is like?"

"Fine, this isn't your locker room where some three-hundred-pound linebacker is waiting for you to turn your head."

I reach over and give him a fist bump. "That's more like it."

"Are you ready for the season?" Harrison asks. I glance over my shoulder and nod.

"I am. I think this will be our year."

"It's definitely your year," my dad adds. "Your mom is itching to start planning a wedding."

"You know it's not up to me, Dad. We wanted Peyton to finish school first and now that she has, I'm sure she'll start planning our wedding. Besides, it's something she'll do with her mom, not mine." I don't know if Peyton has told her parents that she picked out flowers, so I stay quiet there. She told me what they were, but didn't show me pictures. I have no doubt they're gorgeous but will pale in comparison to her on our wedding day.

Quinn starts to choke, which quickly turns to laughter, so does Harrison and my dad. I frown at them all. "You do know that both moms are going to be heavily involved, right?" he states.

I shake my head. The last thing I want to do is add pressure to Peyton. If she wants my mom involved, she'll ask her. Otherwise, Josie Westbury is just going to have to stand on the sidelines. "My mom's just gonna have to wait for Paige to get married."

"She's never getting married," my dad blurts out.

"Unless it's to Mack," Harrison says. My eyes go wide. He has no idea of the conversation that took place at the water tower with Nick and Mack. Everything moves in slow motion, even the rushing rapids have seemed to calm down right now.

"Oh shit," I say as Harrison is chuckling. My dad's head turns slowly, he inhales deeply as his hand, which is holding a can of beer, cocks back. He lets go. The can torpedoes toward Harrison. The thunk from the can hitting Harrison square in the chest can likely be heard by the neighboring campsites. Harrison covers his chest and groans.

"You forget your daughter is marrying my son," my dad seethes. It really should be Harrison reminding my dad of this, since it's my father who has just assaulted my soon-to-be-father-in-law. But that's not how our families work.

"If it were anyone but Noah, I'd have a problem with

it," Harrison says raggedly. I have a feeling my dad's canon of a throw has left a mark on Harrison's chest.

"Do I get to call you dad?" I ask, trying to lighten the mood. I don't think Harrison realizes the severity of his comment about Mack. My dad is already wanting to send Betty Paige to boarding school because of this boy.

Harrison glares at me. "Mr. James will work."

Mr. James? Is he serious?

Quinn spits out the contents of his mouth out and starts choking.

"You okay, son?" Harrison asks.

"Good, good," Quinn answers. "I just didn't expect you to answer like that."

I look straight at Harrison, trying to determine if he's bullshitting me or not. "Are you serious?"

He doubles over, laughing uncontrollably. My dad and Quinn start in as well, as if this is some sort of joke to them. "I'm just kidding," Harrison says. "Don't you think it'd be a bit odd if I made you call me Mr. James?"

"Yes," I tell him.

"And the dad part," Harrison shrugs. "If it's fitting, I don't care really."

The rest of our evening is spent talking about nothing in particular. In fact, most of the time we're quiet and listening to the people next to us, waiting for any sign that they've figured out who is actually on this campsite.

By the time we head into our tent, I'm certain I'm going to ask Quinn tomorrow. Maybe take him out fishing or for another hike. Either way, I want to ask him in private, away from our dads, so he's not pressured to give me an answer he's not comfortable with.

7

PEYTON

To say I'm nervous would be the understatement of the century. I thought Noah's proposal in front of thousands, not counting live television, would've prepared me for anything. But no. Not even close. I swear I'm about to pee my pants from all the shaking I'm doing. Even the tricks I've learned in therapy aren't helping. My palms feel like they're dripping with sweat, and my legs are bouncing so fast the receptionist probably thinks I'm jonesing for my next fix.

"Get yourself together, Peyton. You're better than this," I say to myself, closing my eyes in another attempt to calm down. I have absolutely nothing to lose if this interview doesn't go well, but I also feel like I have everything to gain. Ever since Mr. Bowen called, I've imagined myself breaking down game film with the players and staff. I can see their eyes on me, their pens scribbling furiously over the papers in their notebooks, hands raised with questions, and plays executed like I suggested. Most of all, I see the team winning.

The problem is, I also see Noah. I see him there,

doing what I suggest. I see the other Pioneers clamoring around our living room, listening to what I have to say. Not the Rams. Not ESPN or any of the other news agencies who have offered me jobs.

"Peyton James?" A man dressed in a jet-black suit marches toward me with his hand out. I stand, giving it a firm squeeze. "Leo Bowen. Thank you for coming out on such short notice."

"Well, as you pointed out, I'm not working, so I have time."

"Yet," he says.

"Yet?"

"You're not working yet, which is why we wanted you to come out sooner rather than later, plus the season is about to start and we really want to fill this position with you."

I smile. "That would be great," I tell him for lack of a better response. He asks me to follow him behind the large glass wall. In fact, everything is glass, making me wonder how much they spend on window cleaners every year. The space has an industrial feel. Everything is stainless steel and white, with very few pops of color.

Mr. Bowen leads me into a conference room where a couple of the players and coaches are sitting around a large table. The nerves I had while waiting are back full-force. I swallow hard and smile. Introductions happen, even though I've already figured out who the players are before they say their names. The thought makes me smile and I wonder how proud Noah and Nick would be of me right now.

"Would it be too forward if we asked you to break down a couple of plays for us?" Mr. Bowen asks, pointing at the wall.

That's when I notice the game footage frozen on the screen. I shake my head slowly. "I'll need a few minutes to look at it."

"Be our guest," Deniz Emery says. He's a running back who can't seem to find a gap once he's handed the ball. Any coach should be able to point this out to him. Taking a seat, I start watching the clip, rewinding, taking notes, and rewinding more until I believe I can fix the issue.

"Okay," I say, turning toward the group. I close my eyes briefly and remind myself that I can do this. *This*, breaking down film, is what I love to do with Noah. Doing it for these guys shouldn't be any different.

Picking up the remote, I start the play and talk about what I'm seeing. To me, it seems they're very basic, common mistakes and easily correctable. I go over how Deniz's feet are too wide, that his push-off is slowing him down, making his timing off, which means the gap that was open is already closing by the time he reaches the line of scrimmage again, almost always giving them a loss of yardage. And because I'm a glutton for punishment, I point out that the linemen aren't doing their jobs. That Dua Mellor isn't blocking. When I finish, I set the remote down and wait for a response. Deniz is smiling, but the coaches are slack-jawed, while Mr. Bowen is glaring at his coaching staff.

He finally clears his throat. "Peyton, I have to say, we already knew about Deniz, but Mellor... well, that's something we hadn't noticed yet, which is exactly why we would love to have you on staff here, if you're interested. My secretary is preparing the offer as we speak."

"All because I pointed out a lineman issue?"

"Not just any issue," Deniz speaks up. "I've been

saying this since last season and no one wants to listen to me. I know I'm missing a step, which you so kindly pointed out, but the gap should be open longer than a second. The linemen aren't giving me a chance."

"It's not just the linemen." I turn the video back on and set it to slow motion, pointing out what others are doing and how fast the play breaks down. "I wonder if your count is off. Maybe the cadence needs to be changed."

Leo Bowen throws his pen down onto the table and chuckles. But it's not one of those haha moments. His hands go up in the air. He points at the coaches but says nothing. When he glances at me, his face has softened. "Peyton, clearly we need someone with your objectivity and knowledge on our staff."

Mr. Bowen's secretary walks in and hands him a folder, he promptly slides it in my direction. "Our offer," he says. "Think about it and let me know."

"How much time do I have?"

He fiddles with his pen. "Obviously with the season starting soon, we'd like an answer as soon as possible, but we also recognize that you have a big decision to make. You'll either be on the sidelines as a coach or a reporter."

THE WAVES CRASH against the shore angrily. There's a storm coming, I can feel it in my bones. Another side effect of the accident. I ache, constantly. The cold bothers me so much, and it makes me wonder if standing on the sideline is such a good idea, and I don't like the idea of being stuck in the press box where I wouldn't be able to talk to all the players. Being a reporter, I'd have breaks. I'd be able to seek comfort from the tent, stand by the heater until it's time to go on air. I pull my knees toward my chest, protecting the envelope with my job offer, from blowing away. I came to my parents after the interview, needing to think.

"Don't you want to come inside?" My mom's voice fills me, and the blanket she drapes over my shoulder gives me a bit of warmth. I turn my head slightly as she sits down next to me. "It's so cold out."

"It's going to rain," I point out the obvious.

She nods. "Maybe it'll stay out there, although we need it desperately. The mountains are so dry." Every year the fear of a wildfire threatens, and almost every year one happens because someone wasn't paying attention to their surroundings, forcing people from their homes and wildlife to the beach to seek shelter. Mom turns to me and smiles. She brushes my hair out of my face. "Tell me how today went."

I can't help the smile that spreads across my face, even if my heart is tearing in two. "They offered me the job, with a really nice compensation package."

Her grin matches mine. "That's amazing, Peyton. I'm so proud of you."

"Thanks. Leo Bowen opened my eyes to a job that I didn't know I wanted."

"Oh, I don't know. You were always on the sidelines with Nick when you were younger. I just think that once you joined the school paper, you saw another part of the sports world that you didn't know about. But if you ask me, I think coaching has always been your passion. It was your father's." Mom pauses and turns her attention toward the ocean. It's a long minute of silence between us before she starts speaking again. "He loved it. Coaching and football.

I know you don't remember him much, but each night he'd come home, and you guys would go over game film. He would point everything out to you, and you'd repeat every word. And on Sundays, you'd sit on his lap, watching the games, calling out plays, and throwing your hands up in the air when someone would fumble. The funny part was, you didn't have a team, so you rooted for everyone."

She's right, I don't remember. I don't tell her that though. Sometimes when she talks about my father, I can see the pain in her eyes and the longing in her voice. But then reality hits and I wonder what would've happened if my father hadn't died, and my heart hurts because I love my dad so much, and only know that I do because of what happened when I was five.

"I don't know what to do, Mom. If I take the job, I'd have to move here, and Noah and I would be back to commuting."

"And the other job?"

I shrug. "I commute with that one too, but not as much." I leave out the rest of what's weighing on my mind with that job.

My mom shivers and I move closer to her so we can share the blanket. "You'll make the right decision for you when the time is right."

"Time might be my enemy. The companies who have made job offers want an answer, but I'm waiting for Noah to get back from camping. I want to get his take on everything."

Mom nudges me. "He loves you, Peyton."

I smile so hard my cheeks hurt. "I love him. I always have."

"Geez, do neither of you answer your phones?"

We both turn around to see my sister trudging the last few steps toward us with her phone in her hand. She sits down in front of us, with her back to the ocean. "I've been calling for like," she pauses and looks at her phone. "Twenty minutes."

"Cry me a river," I tell her.

"No thanks, Justin," she smirks. "Tell me what the pow wow is for."

"Peyton was offered the job."

Elle sticks her hand up for a high-five, which I gladly return. "You taking it?"

"I don't know yet, I need to speak to Noah."

"You know he's going to tell you to do what you want," Elle says.

"I know, but he's going to be my husband and I want to discuss it with him."

Elle raises her eyebrow at me. "Speaking of, what's the deal?"

I look from her to my mom and smile. "I picked out the flowers." I show them the pictures I took while in Beaumont. After they look, I take my phone back and glance at them one last time.

"Have you picked a date?" Mom asks.

"Noah has. Well, he's suggested one. Christmas." I look at my mom and sister for their reaction. The timing doesn't seem to faze them. "But I'm not sure. It'll depend on my job. It'll probably be sometime next summer, once the season is over."

Again, Elle and my mom don't say anything. Not that I'd expect them to, but I would like them to give me some thoughts.

"Well, whenever you decide, let me know so I can

clear my schedule. I want to be the best maid of honor ever."

"I haven't asked you yet," I point out.

Elle shrugs. "Are you going to ask someone else?"

I shake my head. "No, but I thought you'd want something formal, like those 'promposals' that everyone's doing."

Her eyes go wide. "Why didn't I think of that?"

My mouth drops open. I was joking, but I think I've just shot myself in the foot.

"Close your mouth. The wind's blowing, and you don't want something disgusting landing in there. Anyway, I want to be your maid of honor, and the last thing I want to do is stress you out. So," she says, letting out an exaggerated exhale. "Let's get to planning your wedding!"

8

NOAH

The bonfire crackles as the sun starts to set over the ocean. All around, family members are talking, carrying on like they haven't seen each other in years, instead of months. For some of us, it's only been weeks. After the camping trip, I went back to Portland to start training, while Peyton stayed at her parents. With the long hours of working out and watching game film, I suggested she stay in California, even though I could've easily used her knowledge and keen eye to make my game better. My girl just knows football. It's one of the qualities I love so much about her.

I look around our little circle and realize how lucky I am. I have teammates whose parents are too old to travel or, for whatever reason, they're not on speaking terms. I can't imagine not talking to my mom or dad on any given day. I still harbor some resentment over the fact my father was missing for the first ten years of my life. I know, it wasn't his fault or my mother's, but the pang of missing important moments with him still lingers.

The women are all gathered together, forming a circle

around my soon to be wife. Each day, I wake and pinch myself, to make sure I'm not dreaming. My life *is* my dream. Peyton and I are going to be married. I want to know the statistics of guys choosing a wedding date because that is where we are right now. I've given her a date, one that I know she wants, but she won't pull the proverbial trigger. I know she doesn't have cold feet, she fears repercussions. I say screw it, and screw them. This is our lives and we should be the only thought when it comes to our wedding. However, the season is approaching fast and I'm going to be tied up, hopefully until the first weekend of February, and I want to be able to help her. I know our moms can handle it, but I want to be a part of making Peyton's fairytale come true. Hell, I want to be Prince Charming and have my fairytale too. I don't want to just show up. It's another dream, leading the Portland Pioneers to the Super Bowl, but not one that's out of reach. Our offseason acquisitions put us high on the depth charts and the rookie sensation we drafted is sure to give us the boost we're going to need to get over the expansion hump.

Their laughter makes me smile. Even from here, I know they're looking at the wedding book Peyton has meticulously put together. Everything from flowers, to dresses and color schemes. Each section of her binder is organized by season. I have yet to fully look through it, I get glimpses when she's sitting beside me and assumes I'm not paying attention to her. The thing is, I'm always watching her, memorizing the way she flips the pages and what season her eyes light up at - Christmas. It's what I want too.

"Do you ever feel like they're talking about you?" Quinn nods toward the group. Not a single one of them is looking around to see if anyone is staring at them. They're too busy oohing and aahing over the collection Peyton is showing them.

"They *are* talking about me," I tell him. "That's Peyton's wedding bible."

"Ah," Quinn says, almost as if he understands. Someday, he will. But until then, I'm just happy he agreed to be my best man. Asking him while we were camping was perfect. Together, with our fishing poles, I poured my heart out to him, telling him how I used to be jealous of the relationship he has with my father. But the more I got to know him, the more it dawned on me that Quinn and I are more alike than we are different. He's my best friend and there isn't anyone else that I want standing up next to me as Peyton, albeit his sister, walks down the aisle toward me.

"Yep," I sigh as I get up, checking to see if Quinn wants something to drink as I head to the cooler. He tells me he's good, but that he'll take one of the cookies sitting out on the tray. Luckily, for me, the cooler is near the love of my life and it gives me an opportunity to be in her presence for a few seconds. It's funny to think I spent most of my life with her, growing up next to her, and yet I can't get enough of her. During the season, the few days we're apart are the hardest of my week. I don't care how many times I'm sacked on Sundays—well I do care, but it's different—missing her is an ache I can't describe. Even though I know I'm going to see her, my heart still breaks each time we have to say goodbye.

I don't want to think about what life will be like if she takes the job here. While she was in Chicago, she didn't have classes every single day so while I was there, we spent time together. Here, things would be different.

She'd travel with the team and we'd be passing each other, most likely in planes, thirty-thousand feet in the air. But if this is the job she wants, she needs to take it and not worry about us. I'll figure that part out because there isn't anything, I wouldn't do for her.

Standing behind Peyton and the rest of the female contingent, I pick up bits and pieces of their conversation. It's my mother who suggests we don't have a winter wedding. My mom knows. She's been around football for a long time. Peyton lets out a dejected sigh and an almost too quiet "I know" that really hits me square in the chest. It seems that I've been clear as mud when it comes to choosing a date and need to really drive the message home that if my girl wants to get married in the winter, I'll make it happen. Even if I have to fake an injury.

"You look lost," my dad says as he stands next to me. "Unless you're admiring."

I laugh because all you can see are the backsides of everyone. "Just listening."

Dad reaches into the cooler and pulls out two beers, handing me one. "Let's take a walk."

"I need to deliver a cookie to Quinn." However, Dad doesn't care and puts his arm on my shoulder, directing me toward the darkened beach. "Is there something wrong?"

"Nope," he says as we trudge through the sand. "Just want to talk to my son for a minute, away from everyone else."

We walk until our feet start to sink into the wet sand from the receding tide. "What's on your mind?"

He laughs. "Not mine, yours. I wasn't kidding when I said you looked lost back there. What's going on?"

I sigh heavily and take a quick drink from the bottle of

beer. Not my favorite, but right now I don't care. "Peyton wants a Christmas wedding but is fearful of the backlash. Not only from the league and players but future employers. I've tried telling her none of that matters, but she's worried about my image and how she will be perceived."

Dad is silent as we stand there listening to the ocean as it laps at the shore. For the most part, the beach is private, and the only people out here are the homeowners. Long put away are the pile of surf and wakeboards we had out earlier. Even though it stormed weeks ago, Quinn was still insistent that we hit the waves.

"So why not just propose the date to her?"

"I have."

"Try harder," he smirks. Such a wise, smart-ass, man.

LATER THAT NIGHT, Peyton and I lie in bed, facing each other. It's times like this when I wish we had rented a hotel room, but her parents would be hurt. Of course, I should be thankful they allow me to stay the night with her. I think they know if I weren't allowed, she wouldn't stay here.

"You looked like you were having a good time going through your book tonight."

"I was," she says. "It's nice to be here with everyone instead of exchanging emails about ideas. Where did you go with your dad?"

"You noticed?"

"I always notice, Noah. As soon as you started walking away, I knew."

I slide a bit closer to her. "Did you watch me walk away?" I ask, teasing her.

Thankfully, the moonlight is beaming through the window because without it, I wouldn't be able to tell she's blushing. I run my thumb over the pinkness of her cheek and smile. "I love you."

"I love you too."

"Tell me what you want, Peyton. You know I'll give it to you." She doesn't say anything, although I can see it in her eyes; she has so much to say. "Will you marry me?" I ask her.

Peyton grins. "I've already said yes, a few times. You don't have to keep asking me again. I'm not going to change my mind."

I inch closer and rest my hand on her hip. "I wasn't finished with my question. Peyton, will you marry me on Christmas Day in front of our friends and family in the same church where my parents were married?" I leave out the part where we mourned her father so many years ago.

"Noah?"

"It's a Tuesday, Peyton. I know this is what you want. A Christmas wedding. I see your face light up each time you're looking through your winter section. And as it turns out, we'll have a bye the following weekend so we can go away for a few days. Our honeymoon won't be much, but we'll be together. The only thing that I don't know, that I can't tell you about is your schedule and what you will do. But with Christmas being a Tuesday, surely you'd be off."

"Are you sure, Noah? Your teammates, they'll talk. My future employer..."

"Without a doubt, Peyton. I just want to marry you and if you want a Christmas wedding, we'll make it happen."

Peyton launches herself forward and presses her lips

to mine. "I love you so much," she says against my lips. "You have no idea."

"I think I do," I tell her as I pull her tight to my body. As much as I want to make love to her, we can't. I won't disrespect her parents in their home. Instead, we make out like teenagers, pausing only to talk about wedding plans.

"I have to make a decision about a job."

"Or you don't," I tell her. "No one will fault you for taking more time for yourself, or even taking time to plan your wedding."

Peyton runs her fingers through my hair. "The offer from the Rams is really nice, but the distance—"

"We'd make it work if it's what you wanted."

She lays her head down on my chest and drags her fingers lazily over my skin. I hold her tight, wishing I could make things easy for us. It's like we've been dealt one blow after another and we haven't even started our lives together as husband and wife yet.

THE LOUD SHRILL of my phone ringing rouses me from sleep. I reach for it and realize that Peyton's no longer in bed. "Hello?"

"Did I wake you?" Bud Walter's booming voice echoes through the receiver.

"No... sort of. What's up?" I ask my coach.

"Be here in an hour, we need to talk."

"I'm in California. I can meet tomorrow," I tell him, sitting up and rubbing the sleepiness away from my face. I'm exhausted and wonder what time it is. Peyton and I were up all night talking about the wedding. Things were going well until I suggested Santa Claus marry us and that we have elves for ushers.

"Westbury, I can't stress enough how important it is that you get here, now."

"What's going on, Coach?"

He sighs. It's loud and sounds disgruntled. He jostles the phone and then clears his throat. "Sorry, I needed to move rooms. Listen, I don't know what you're doing there, but the owners got wind that you're shopping yourself to the Rams and they're pissed. They thought you liked it here and were going to sign an extension. I did too."

My heart drops. I don't want to think the worst, but I am. If the Rams are using Peyton to get to me, they'll be sorry for hurting her. I'll make sure of it, and if I lose my job because of them, I'll sue them.

"Look, I don't know what's going on, but I haven't met with the Rams or anyone. My fiancée... they offered her a job a few weeks back, that's it."

"Unfortunately, the newswire has a different story. Just get here, Westbury, the sooner, the better." He hangs up, leaving me with nothing but an agonizing feeling. I'm going to lose my job.

I get dressed, throw my clothes in my suitcase, send an urgent text to my dad that I need the plane, and walk out into the living room to find Peyton, her mom, and sister hovering over piles of magazines.

"Hey, babe," she says when she sees me. The smile she has quickly faded once she notices my bags. "Are you leaving?"

"The Rams..." I pause and think hard about how I should approach this. I don't want her to feel used, but that's exactly how things look. "I have to go back to Portland and meet with the staff. Someone is saying that I'm shopping the Rams for an offer."

Peyton stands, the mortification of my words evident on her face. "We never even spoke about you in the interview."

I nod. "I know."

"Are you getting cut?"

I shake my head slightly. "I need to go and do damage control."

"Harrison is outside, Noah. I'll have him drive you to the airfield," Katelyn scrambles toward the door as Peyton comes toward me.

"That's such shit," Elle blurts out. "Peyton doesn't need you to get a job."

"Elle," Peyton scolds.

"She's right, you don't need me. I don't think the Rams got that message though." I hate saying it, but why else would they spread the rumor that I'm meeting with them? They have to know this isn't how you go after someone whose contract is coming due. "I have to go," I tell Peyton, who's on the verge of tears. I lean down and kiss her. "I love you."

I have to force myself to leave her standing there, knowing she's about to break down. Her sister is there, and as angry as Elle is, she'll take care of Peyton while I'm gone.

9

PEYTON

*H*ave you ever felt your life start to slip through your fingers? I'm not talking about dying, but the life you envisioned yourself having? For me, I've always dreamed of being Noah's wife, having his children, and growing old with him. Being by his side while he played football or baseball, loving him until I stopped breathing.

This is how I felt when Noah told me what the Rams did to him, to me...to us, like I was dying. Hurting Noah is the last thing I would ever do. As soon as the words sunk in, I immediately called and told them I wouldn't be accepting the job. I did so without hesitation. I would never want to jeopardize Noah's career. There isn't a job out there that would make me choose them over him. Ever.

And I feel useless and used. I never would've thought a team would do something like this to get to Noah, to try and ruin his career, to get his attention. There are better ways, procedures that protect everyone. That's what really gets me, the fact they started spreading rumors that would surely get him into trouble with the Pioneers, making sure he'd never play for them. I don't get it.

What also bothers me, tears me up inside, is that the Rams gave me a different outlook on my job situation. They offered me something I love to do, something that I'm good at, only to get to Noah, and it's made me question everything. Am I good enough to be a sideline reporter? Broadcaster? A wife to Noah? He knows about my insecurities and assures me that nothing will change between us. But I feel like it already has.

He's gone before I wake up, and home after I've gone to bed. I know it's stupid to think, but I wonder if he's waiting down on the street for me to turn off the lights before he finally comes home so he can avoid talking to me. He holds me while we're asleep, but he's restless. Tossing and turning, thrashing about while he dreams. All I want is for him to tell me what's going on, how he's feeling. Yell at me for being stupid, even though it wasn't my fault. I just want him to be present, to come back to me, and I know that I can't wait for that to happen. I need to take this head-on. We're getting married in a few months and I don't want to wonder if my groom's ready or not as I walk down the aisle.

The ride over to the practice facility takes longer than I planned. We're stuck in traffic and I fear I'm going to miss practice. When we reach the source of the jam, my stomach twists and turns. There's an accident. A mangled car is being loaded onto the back of a tow truck, and there's glass everywhere. The only people at the scene are the clean-up crew and probably the investigator. I've often wondered what the scene of my accident looked like. I could look pictures up on the web, go back to the police department and see the photos, but I'm not sure I could handle it.

My nerves were already on edge, but now they're frayed. I should've asked Noah if it were okay for me to come and watch him today. This year the Pioneers are holding a mini-camp before training camp officially starts in the middle of July. The popularity of the team is such that the marketing group is trying to make the team more accessible to the younger crowd. Last year, the stands at the practice facility were so jam-packed with people, that some complained. The owners didn't like that much and asked the players what they thought about doing something for the fans. From what I understand, mostly everyone was on board.

The camp is open to everyone, and the public's encouraged to attend. For some, this is their only chance to see their favorite players since ticket prices are outrageous, and the Pioneers tend to sell-out, especially when the more popular teams come to town. Often, in between sessions, the players will sign autographs and pose for photos. The fans love it. Noah once said that this is the way he builds his fan base. It doesn't matter how tired or sore he is, he won't pass up the opportunity to pose, especially if the fan is younger.

The Players Association limits what the guys can do though. The rules are strict, with the big one being no contact. Still, the defensive line likes to tease Noah that they're coming after him.

By the time the car service pulls into the parking lot, I'm second-guessing everything and wondering if I should go home and wait. Wait for what, though, I don't know. He won't be home until late and waiting up for him has proved futile in the past. If I'm asleep on the couch, he'll carry me to bed, and for some reason, I'm so exhausted I never wake-up.

I feel like I'm about to heave my breakfast and lunch. It's stupid really considering the only thing I'm doing is going to watch my fiancé throw the football around. And talk to him. I'm going to force him to speak to me, whether he likes it or not. I have to know where his head is. I must know that we're on the same page.

There are a few familiar faces passing by as I walk toward the field, which puts me at ease. I don't know of any other wives or girlfriends attending the mini-camp, so I'm pleased to see I'm not the only one who ventured out today.

"Peyton!" I look for the voice calling my name and smile at Alex Moore's girlfriend, Maggie. They've been together for a little over a year and seem to be doing well. I go over to her, she takes my hands and squeezes them. "How are the wedding plans coming?"

"Good," I tell her as I sit down. "Everything is coming along swimmingly." Minus the fact that I fear my fiancé doesn't want to get married anymore and I don't have a dress or chosen my bridesmaids. But who's really keeping track?

"Alex was surprised that Noah asked him to be in the wedding."

I look at her quickly before turning my attention back to the field. I can't let her know that I had no idea Noah did that. It would make sense though. Alex and Noah have been friends for a long time, and I suspected he wants Alex to be there. "Does Alex look good in brown?" I ask her.

Maggie's eyes go wide. "Not going the traditional route?"

"There's nothing traditional about Noah and me. Besides, all the men in our lives have to wear tuxes a lot. Our dads for the events they go to, the team for the galas. I wanted to give them a reprieve."

She bumps her shoulder with mine. "That's very nice of you, and they'll appreciate it. What about you. Have you picked your dress? Colors?"

Shaking my head slightly, I scan the field for Noah. When I spot him, my heart begins to race. He's on the far sideline, his hands are clutching his jersey, and he's speaking to his offensive coordinator.

"Peyton?"

I startle and smile. "Sorry, I got lost in thought." More like lost in a vision. "I haven't found a dress yet. My sister is pestering me to go on Say Yes To The Dress, but I'm not sure that's my thing. We live such public lives that I'd like our wedding to be somewhat private."

"That makes a ton of sense. If I can help, let me know."

"Thank you, Maggie."

When I first met her, I felt sorry for her. Here she was, a children's museum director, thrust into the spotlight without any warning. Alex had invited her to dinner. Told her to wear something fancy. The big oaf didn't tell her that he was taking her to the annual hospital fundraiser and that she'd be mobbed by cameras the moment she stepped out of the car. She shook with nerves all night at dinner and I did my best to ease her, but she still had the look of a deer caught in headlights, waiting for impact. Luckily for Alex, she agreed to a second date. This time, it was much more low-key, with Noah and me.

Noah takes the field, effectively cutting off any conversation between Maggie and myself. Of course, where Noah is, Alex is as well. The two are never far from each other. Alex protects Noah, it's his job, and while any practice prohibits the defense from touching Noah, Alex still takes his job very seriously.

The whistle blows and my quarterback takes center, looks to his left and then right while calling his cadence. I can barely hear him over the crowd, mostly young children screaming Noah's name. The pat on Alex's thigh is subtle, but I notice, and that's when I see the hesitation in Noah's hands, followed by three steps back. Not his usual five. He fires a pass across the center of the field, hitting cornerback Cameron Simmons right in the chest. The spiral is perfect. The crowd cheers. I look at Noah, waiting for his reaction. There's nothing. He's not rushing to the line of scrimmage even though there's under two minutes left and according to the clock, he's losing. It's not real, at least the score isn't. But that doesn't negate that Noah should be taking this seriously. Practice is practice, everyone needs it.

He finally gets back to the line of scrimmage. Everything repeats except the route changed. This time, he hands off to Terry Price, a seasoned running back and offseason acquisition. Price weaves through the line, bringing in almost twenty yards. The defensive coordinator is losing his shit on the sideline. It's funny, at least for the time being. For this being a mini-camp, the staff is certainly invested.

Three more plays later and Noah throws the ball to Julius Cunningham for a touchdown. There's no pomp or circumstance with this, but it's still an achievement of sorts. Noah heads to the sideline and the rookie quarterback takes over. I would think being a camp for the fans, Noah would play the entire time. My heart plummets, thinking that Noah's playing time is being affected by the bullshit with the Rams.

Noah sits on the bench and hangs his head, letting his helmet dangle from his fingers. I'm confused by this. His set was good, it resulted in a touchdown.

Against my better judgment, I head over to the other side of the field and stand behind him. "What's your problem, Westbury?" I yell rather loudly to get his attention. He turns. At first, his expression is one of anger, almost as if he's pissed someone asked him this question. When his eyes settle on me, I give him a little wave and he comes right over. The jitters I was experiencing before I arrived are back, tenfold. I don't know what he's going to say or how he's going to react to me being here.

I get my answer as soon as he reaches me. He slides his hands through the railings and pulls me as close as he can to him. I wish I had just walked onto the field. I'm allowed but didn't know how he'd feel about it.

"What's wrong, Noah?" I ask, leaning down to whisper in his ear.

He shakes his head, pushing deeper into my stomach. "Nothing feels right."

I hold him as best as I can. I did this to him. Well, not me, but the Rams. They were underhanded and put him in a bad spot with the team and the owners. Noah would never do anything to jeopardize his spot on the team. My accident notwithstanding.

"It's only a mini-camp," I remind him.

"That doesn't matter. Not this year."

He's right, it doesn't. This is on me, my fault. Not purposefully, but still. And I have to do what I can to fix this mess. "How can I help?"

He looks at me, and I'm tempted to lean over and give

him a kiss. I miss the way his lips feel against mine. "Tell me what I'm doing wrong. Yell at me. I'm afraid I'm going to lose my starting job to..." Noah turns quiet. He doesn't have to say it. I nod and run my finger through his damp hair, not caring about the sweat.

I love that he takes his job so seriously. "I got you, Westbury." I wink, and he lets go of me. Instead of sitting down, I stay at the railing, giving me a better angle. He takes the field. I focus on him, not the play, not the team, just Noah. Again, I notice that his hands are hesitant, almost as if he's unsure of the play he's running. My first thought is he has a concussion and hasn't told anyone. And then I watch his feet. It's a different play from before. Three steps, not five. Last year, every play he ran, he took those extra two steps.

"Five steps," I mumble to myself. "It's always five. Why change it?"

"Because the new offensive coordinator thinks Noah's more powerful off three."

The general manager of the Pioneers leans on the railing next to me. He's watching the play unfold on the field, while I study him. Weeks ago, he wanted to fire my guy, all because of a nasty rumor.

"Noah's always done five," I point out. "He's been successful with that rhythm."

He shrugs. "Coaches feel otherwise."

"I see." I bite my tongue on what I really want to say. The last thing I want to do is put Noah in any more hot water. I turn and take a seat on the first bleacher and slouch a bit, so I can still watch. The GM follows, making me feel uneasy.

He sits down and sighs. "The Rams are fools."

I smile but say nothing.

"They thought by luring you, they'd lure him. What they didn't count on, was his loyalty."

"Noah's very loyal."

"And you're right about him." He points to Noah.

"I'm sorry."

"Look, Ms. James. We can't offer you what the Rams threw at you, but we can offer you a job. Same position, player analysis."

"Why?" I ask.

This time he points to the offensive coordinator. "Alton Rennie."

"I'm sorry, but the name doesn't ring a bell, other than him working for the Pioneers."

"He's good friends with Nick Ashford, who speaks very highly of you. When everything happened with the Rams, he said we'd be stupid not to offer you something. He loves Noah and wants to keep him. We do as well. Hell, we want the both of you. We know what you've done for him, Alex and Julius." This man, the one who can ruin Noah's career, looks at me.

"And if Noah wasn't my fiancé?"

He nods toward Rennie again. "Wouldn't make any difference. He wants you. Says you'll be an asset. I imagine once word spreads about the Rams, we would've followed suit anyway. We'd be stupid not too. As will other teams that will seek you out. Think about it, Ms. James, and let me know." He walks away, leaving the offer to work for the Pioneers in mid-air, and leaving me with another major decision.

NOAH

*T*he water from the shower turns cold in no time. It's karma and not the shitty water system the practice facility has. At least that's what I'm telling myself. Over the past few weeks, I haven't been a good boyfriend, fiancé, teammate or much of anything. I let my own thoughts get in the way of what really matters, playing football and marrying Peyton. Stupidly, I let something out of her control dictate my feelings, and I took it out on her, making sure to avoid her as much as possible. Not because I'm mad at her, because I'm not. What the Rams did to her is inexcusable. I'm pissed because they used her to get to me. They dangled an enticing job offer out in front of her, let her believe they were interested in her, only to start coming after me. Which, honestly, makes no sense. Their QB is good and riding the pine as a back-up isn't something I'm interested in, so why they would think this, is beyond me. More so, I'm angry that they made Peyton feel like I'm the only way she can get a job. Her abilities far outreach mine. I can throw a ball and read a defense. But Peyton, she sees the whole game. She's better than I am. They would know that if they actually paid attention.

I fully expect Peyton to be gone by the time I drag my sorry ass out of the gym. There are a few fans waiting for autographs. I start signing as I walk toward the parking lot. It's when I see Peyton, leaning up against our car, with her legs crossed at her ankles and her hands resting inside her pockets that I tell the remainder of the people that I'm in a hurry and to come back tomorrow.

Rushing the last few steps, I drop my bag and place my hands on her cheeks, pulling her forward until our lips are pressed together. I deepen the kiss, not caring about the onlookers. They can happily take pictures, and send them to me, I wouldn't mind.

"Wow," she says when we pull away. Our foreheads are touching, and both of us are breathless. I can't believe I went weeks without kissing her like this, or that she allowed it after the way I've treated her. I hate to say it, but maybe some ground rules need to be set: If Noah's acting like an ass, Peyton has every right to kick him where the sun don't shine. That's what she did this time, more or less.

"I'm sorry for acting like a dick."

"I know you are," she says, running her fingers down the side of my cheek. "Are you ready to go home?"

I nod and walk her around to the passenger side of the car. Once she's settled, I stow my bag and climb in. "Peyton," I say as I turn the key. "I called Allen."

"Probably smart," she says, although she has no idea why I called my agent. "It's better to keep him informed."

"It's not that." I pull out of the parking lot and into

traffic, heading in the opposite direction to our apartment. I reach for her hand and bring it to my lips, kissing her ring. I can't wait to place her wedding band there, to seal our future with the vows I've written for her. "I asked him to look into possible baseball teams. Teams that might need a pitcher at the lower level."

I can feel her eyes on me, but I refuse to look away from the road. Not only for safety reasons but because I don't want to see her expression.

"Why would you do that?"

I half shrug. "To give you a fighting chance." As soon as the words are out of my mouth, I regret them. I turn to look at her, turning the wheel as I do. She hollers at me and clutches my arm until I've righted the car. I do what's best for both of us and turn down a side street to pull over.

With the car idling, I shift in my seat to look at her. Peyton's staring straight ahead, lips pursed, and fuming. I know I've insulted her, but that wasn't my intention. "Hear me out, babe. I called Allen and asked about potential teams because I want you to follow *your* dreams in broadcasting football. It's been your passion for as long as I can remember. When I wanted to quit, you're the one who encouraged me to stick it out. As much as football means to me, it means more to you. I know this. I know that this is your way of hanging onto a piece of your father, and the last thing I want to do is take that away from you. And if that means I let it go, so be it."

Peyton wipes at her cheek. Great, I've made her cry. That's the last thing I've wanted to do. I push her hair away from her face and past her shoulder and try to guide her to me, but she's stiff, unmoving. To say I'm in the doghouse would be an understatement. I should've kept my mouth shut, but I was worried that Allen would call or show up with some news, which would piss her off because I didn't tell her. My reasoning for calling my agent though, that's probably not the best.

"Peyton, I'm sorry. I thought I was trying to help."

"It's not that."

Color me confused. "Okay, so what is it?"

She turns, her tear streaked face breaks my heart. I use my thumbs to wipe at the makeup running down her cheeks. "Logan Baker offered me a job."

My hand pauses, my thumbs holding tight against her cheeks. "*My* Logan Baker?"

She half laughs, half coughs. "Do you have something going on with Logan?"

I shake my head. "Lately, I prefer to stay far away from him."

"I think he's afraid to lose you. He offered me the same job and says it's because of Alton Rennie."

"Alton Rennie?"

She nods. "He knows Nick, and I guess Nick has a lot of nice things to say about me."

I finally drop my hands as I have a lightbulb moment. "Alton... this all makes sense."

"What does?"

"I couldn't remember where I knew him from or why he was riding my ass so hard about my steps. It's something Nick used to get on me about, taking too long in the pocket or getting too far away from protection. I don't know why, but the five has always been my thing."

"Because it was your dad's."

She's right. I used to watch DVDs of him playing, long before I knew he was my dad. I wanted to be like the great Liam Westbury. Play like him, be him. "Nick used to harp on me. In high school, he brought in this specialist – Ren. They tried to change my footwork, but I refused."

"Alton Rennie," she whispers while I nod. "He told Logan to hire me."

I sit back and look out the window. Peyton working for the Pioneers. I sort of like the idea. "But, why? Not that I don't think you'd be amazing."

"I don't know. Logan didn't say much, just that they can't offer me the same package, but I'd have the same position. He said Alton told him he'd be stupid not to hire me."

Finally, I turn and look at the love of my life. "What are you going to tell them?"

"How would you feel about me being there, every day? I'd be paid to point out what you're doing wrong, where the defense is breaking down."

"Remember it was just mini-camp."

Peyton shrugs. "I notice everything, especially when you're playing."

"I think you should take the job."

"Are you sure, Noah? This would mean we'd have zero separation. I'd travel with the team."

I waggle my eyebrows at her. "I wonder if they'd let us share a hotel room?"

Peyton slaps my arm. "Be honest with me."

Leaning over, I cup the back of her neck and pull her toward me. Our lips hover closely. "Take the job, Peyton." I pull away, putting some space between us so I can talk to her. "You might as well get paid to tell me when I suck instead of yelling at me after the game. Besides, I can't get mad at you this way."

She looks at me confusingly. "Have you ever gotten mad at me before?"

Nope, she's got me there. "No, I haven't because you're always honest and would never say anything that wasn't true. Still, I think you should take the job."

"And what if you get traded?"

I grin quickly. Being traded isn't something I ever want to think about. "Then we commute, just like we would now if you were to take one of the broadcasting jobs."

"Okay."

"Okay?"

"I'm going to do it."

A smile breaks out across my face as we meet in the middle. Having her at work with me every day is going to be an adjustment, but I'd rather it be her than anyone else. I like to think I'm easy to coach, but I know I can be stubborn. Peyton won't take that shit from me. She'll happily put me in my place and not think twice about it.

I put the car into drive and pull back onto the main road. We drive for a while, listening to sports talk radio, which I have to say, with Peyton is never fun. She yells back at whoever is hosting, pointing out how wrong, and sometimes how right, they are. And will go as far as to throw her hands up in the air when she's completely frustrated. It's comical, and her antics will undoubtedly make the ESPN highlight reel.

She's going to have to let the stations down easily though. The last thing she wants to do is burn bridges. While she might like working for the Pioneers, broadcasting is what she went to school for, and I'd hate to see her pass up a future opportunity.

"I spoke with Maggie today. She says you asked Alex to be in the wedding?"

"Sort of. It was more like Alex asking who my best

man was and when I told him it was Quinn, he said he was okay with that and preferred walking all the women to their seats. I couldn't really tell him no at that point. Is that okay?"

"It's your wedding too, Noah. Of course, it's okay. I suppose we should figure out the rest of the party though."

"We should have a massive reception."

"Doable. Our families do like to party."

"That they do," I say as I turn into a parking lot. Peyton's never been here, but I've talked to her about it. We're at the top of Portland, overlooking the city. The sun is setting, making this moment just about perfect.

I get out of the car, rush to her side, and take her hand in mine. Together, we walk to the edge. With me standing behind her, I wrap her in my arms. "This is our city, Peyton. From here, we can see everything."

"It's gorgeous, Noah."

We stand there for a while, me holding her. I want to tell her how much I love her, thank her for being my constant, my go-to, for being my best friend. I need to apologize for being a jerk to her for weeks on end, for avoiding the elephant in the room, for likely making her feel as if she's done something wrong. It's a Westbury trait, getting inside your own head, and it takes a really strong woman to help us see the error of our ways. That's what Peyton did for me today when she showed up at practice. If she hadn't, I don't know where I'd be right now, probably wandering around aimlessly downtown, waiting for her to go to bed because I was too ashamed to face her with what I had done.

Peyton turns her head slightly to look up at me. I lean

down and kiss the tip of her nose. "What's on your mind?" I ask her.

"I'm really happy, Noah."

"I am too, babe."

"Then why have you been ignoring me for the past few weeks?"

I go to step back, but she holds on to my arms, digging her nails into my flesh.

"Don't," she says. "Don't move, turn, walk or think about leaving until you tell me why. Is it because of the Rams?"

My head moves slowly up and down. "I got scared, Peyton. I thought I was going to lose everything and you at the same time."

"How do you think I felt?"

"Probably the same as me. But the only way I knew how to cope with it was to work my ass off. I wanted everyone to see how committed I was to the team. I showed up at the facility before it opened and was there when the janitor locked up at night."

"So, you weren't waiting until I turned out the lights and was asleep before you came in?"

I lean back and look at her. "What? Hell no. I'd much rather be with you, but I didn't, still don't, want to lose my job."

Peyton looks down and lessens her grip on my arms. As gently as possible, I lift her chin until her eyes are meeting mine. "What's going on in that pretty head of yours?"

"I thought you were avoiding me because of the Rams. It's why I came out to see you today."

"My beautiful, silly girl. You are perfect. You're the

love of my life. There isn't anything you could do to make me walk away from you. Ever."

"I'm sorry about the Rams, about everything."

"Don't. Don't apologize for their arrogance. I love you, Peyton, and no job will ever change that."

PEYTON

*B*y the time we stop at the third bridal store, or maybe it's the fourth, could be fifth because I've lost count, I realize why couples elope. The stress of having everything right, everything perfect, is almost too much to handle. The words I've heard today are it's too frilly, not enough lace, the back looks odd, you look frumpy, is enough to make me want to throw my hands up and say forget it. Maybe it's the champagne talking and being unreasonable in my head. With each store, comes a plate of hors d'oeuvres from restaurants looking to land a contract from me, and champagne from the best vineyards wanting to supply our reception with their bottles. Because of my dad and who I'm marrying, the A-list treatment is real and all I want to do is pick a wedding dress with my mom and sister and decide on bridesmaids' gowns that don't look like they belong in an 80s prom magazine. Most of all, I just want to marry Noah, in front of our family and friends, in a simple ceremony.

I'm surrounded by mirrors, and my reflection tells me that I'm tired and have had way too much champagne. I want to eat, gorge myself on carbs and ice cream until my stomach revolts. I want everything unhealthy and not listed on the approved list that my uncle Xander gave me. He means well and is only giving me what I wanted when I asked him to help get me into shape for my wedding.

My body jerks to the left or right, depending on which way the saleswoman is pulling the gown I'm trying on. It's not my favorite, but my mom fawned over it as soon as she saw it on the hanger. In fact, she's loved just about every dress she's picked out, as well as some of Elle's choices. Each one I show her brings her to tears. I guess this is a mom thing to do, to cry at the sight of their daughters dressed in wedding gowns. I texted Noah and warned him I plan to be the same way when we have a daughter going through this. He replied, telling me how much he loves the idea that we're going to have children.

I have yet to find the *one*. Not man, because I found him many years ago, but dress. In my mind, it exists. It's out there, sitting on some rack, being passed by, waiting for me to try it on. I know I could have had a bespoke gown, designed, and made to my own specifications if I were to delay my wedding for a few more months. I'm not sure a dress is worth it. My parents are going to spend hundreds, if not thousands, on a dress that I'll wear for a few hours, send off to dry-cleaning and have stored in a box. It seems frivolous and a waste of someone's time.

Elle enters the dressing area and crinkles her nose. She gets it. At least, she pretends to. "Do you like it?"

I stare at her through the mirrors, not answering. I don't need to. It's a twin thing, she knows how I'm feeling.

"Mom means well. She's excited."

"I can't wait for it to be your turn," I tell her. "When will Ben propose?"

Elle shrugs, playing my question off. Her relationship with Ben is similar to the one I share with Noah. Lifelong loves with the difference being Elle didn't realize she was in love with Ben until it was almost too late. Her stubbornness almost blew her chance at happiness, but thankfully Ben was determined to win her love.

"What? Don't you talk about marriage?"

"Not really," she says. "We're both so busy. Ben has a really good job, plus he's helping me launch my career. We're both sort of focusing on work right now."

"You want him to ask you. I can tell."

Elle waves me off. "The commitment would be nice."

"So ask *him*. I would've had Noah not. I wasn't going to let him go."

The saleswoman makes one final tug before she dismisses me to go see my mom. Elle helps me off the large platform and holds the curtains open for me. Mom stands, covers her mouth, and proudly proclaims this is the best one yet.

"Mom, you say that each time," Elle points out. "How are we supposed to help Peyton choose?"

Mom wipes at the tears falling. "I can't help it, I just..." She looks from me to Elle, and then down at the floor. "I'm emotional is all."

She doesn't have to finish her sentence. I already know she was going to say something like "never thought she'd see this day." She's not the only one to think that. Sometimes, I have nightmares about the wedding, about Noah and I. Me sitting in church, watching him marry someone else. I'm there out of obligation because our families have been friends for forever. In this dream, his bride finds me crying in the bathroom, telling me that everything will be okay. She has no idea who I am or that

I'm madly in love with her new husband. She just sees a weeping woman in the restroom who needs comfort. When my dreams do show my wedding to Noah, it's perfect because it's him and I standing there, professing our love for one another.

"Peyton, do you like the dress?" my mother asks.

I look down and trace the intricate beadwork. A seamstress or tailor spent a long time putting this together and it will be the right dress for a bride that isn't me. "It's pretty, but I think it's too busy for what I had in mind."

Mom smiles. "We have a handful of other stores to try."

"Actually, there's a vintage shop not far from here. I'd like to look in there."

She nods. I can't tell if she's dejected or not. She goes back to where she was sitting and starts gathering her stuff. Elle tugs on my arm, directing me toward the dressing room. I have to stand there and wait for my salesperson to come back, and when she does, she has a fake smile on her face. I get it, she just lost a sale. In all fairness, so did the other stores we visited earlier.

As soon as we leave, Elle tells us that we're walking the few blocks to the other store. It's nice out, perfect actually. It's not too hot, there's a light breeze and the sun is shining. Elle and I walk hand in hand while Mom trails behind us, talking to our dad on the phone. From the bits and pieces of their conversation, she tells him that everything is going great and that we are weighing our options on a few dresses. I think she too has had too much champagne.

Halfway to the shop, we get noticed. Normally, we can walk the streets, and no one pays attention unless our dad, one of our uncles, Noah or sometimes Quinn is with us. Most often, the paparazzi doesn't care about Elle or me or our mother unless she's shopping with our aunts. But Elle has started a band, and they're starting to get a little bit of attention. And I'm marrying a famous quarterback, who publicly asked me to marry him. And I'm certain one of the shops we visited has alerted the media about what I'm doing today because on the sidewalk, coming toward us is a mob of photographers. By mob, I mean a few, but they're screaming and rushing toward us, making me feel uncomfortable.

For the most part, our run-ins with the media have been controlled. Growing up in Beaumont kept us out of the limelight, unlike a few of our famous friends. But even when we were on tour with the band, we had security with us and for the most part, the photographers would keep their distance.

Today, not so much.

Questions are being yelled. They want to know if I'm pregnant, when the wedding is, and they're asking Elle who Quinn's girlfriend is. That question gives me pause, even though our mother is pushing us toward the store. She tells them that we have no comment and to leave us alone, which I think only furthers their agenda in getting answers. Someone brings up Dessie and I pause, but Elle tells them to leave us alone and puts her arm around me.

For whatever reason, Dessie is still a sore subject with me, and I don't know why. In the end, I have my guy and we're getting married, but part of me still harbors some resentment toward her. In the beginning of their relationship, she had no idea how I felt about him and neither did he. By the end, she knew I was the demise and did the unthinkable. I don't know if Noah will ever get over the betrayal. I know I won't. Yet, I can't shake the feeling that she's lingering in the shadows, waiting to pounce again. It's stupid, Elle tells me this all the time. I know that Noah loves me.

The manager of the dress shop hurries toward us, shutting and locking the door. "Phew," she says, leaning up against it. "This is the second day in a row I've had to lock the door because of the photographers. You celebs sure know how to keep things interesting."

"We're not famous," I tell her.

"You must be to them. I'm Claudia, the owner." She comes forward and shakes our hands.

"I'm Peyton, this is my sister Elle and our mother, Katelyn."

"It's nice to meet you. Who's the bride?"

Elle points at me. "She is."

Claudia smiles and takes my arm to lead me toward her dresses. "I'm sure you're aware we specialize in the vintage look. Everything is handmade, and we do all the alterations on site. When's your wedding?"

"Christmas."

"Day?"

I nod.

"Doable. Do you know what you're looking for?"

"I do." Unlike the other stores, Claudia and I go through the dresses while Mom and Elle stay in the background. I tell Claudia how I imagine my dress, what my theme is, and the colors Noah and I have chosen. I think she was shocked to find out that we're not going with red, like most winter weddings. Within a few minutes, she has me set up in the dressing area with a handful of dresses.

As soon as I step out onto the pedestal, I look at myself in the mirror while she zips me up. She's prattling on about the fabric, but I'm lost in a sea of visions. Me standing next to Noah, holding his hand. The two of us, side-by-side, posing for pictures. Me with my arms around him while we dance at our reception.

"What do you think?" Claudia asks, standing next to me.

"This is the one." *This is the one.* This dress is everything I was looking for but didn't know I wanted until I saw what I looked like in the mirror. I move my hips back and forth to watch the tiered skirt twist. It reminds me of Cinderella, just without the lace. The satin fabric is exactly what I wanted, and the small bow in front is just enough to give the simple, yet classic ballgown enough character. I'm in love with the capped sleeves. I didn't know I wanted those until now. I run my hands down the front, loving that Noah can hold me without worrying whether his suit is going to get caught on my dress. The train length is perfect. It'll cover the church stairs but won't be bothersome during the reception. Turning slightly, the tiers cascade elegantly, making me fall more in love.

"Let's go show your mom and sister."

Claudia holds back the large curtain separating the dressing room from the store. I step through, both Mom and Elle gasp. I'm watching Mom though because every dress earlier has made her cry and I fully expect the same reaction. This time, she covers her mouth and shakes her head before she starts fanning herself.

"I can't, Peyton."

"Can't what?" I ask her.

"Find the words. You were right. Everything from before... they pale in comparison. You look stunning."

The smile on my face is going to last me until well after my wedding day. I glance at Elle. She's crying.

"You're so beautiful," she says as she comes to me. "I think you should curl your hair but leave it down. Maybe pull a few strands back, like this." I can't see what she's doing, but Mom and Claudia are nodding.

"We'll take the dress," Mom says.

"Do you want to know the price?"

Mom shakes her head. "It doesn't matter, I'd pay millions to see her light up like this every day."

As fast as I can, I move to my mom to give her a hug. "Thank you, Mom."

"Thank you for staying," she whispers into my ear. The magnitude of her words sends my heart and the rest of my body into some sort of frenzied motion. I'm shaking, on the verge of tears as she cups my face and tells me that she loves me. I'm also speechless, unsure how to respond. Do I tell her she's welcome? Of course not, that's not the right answer. Maybe, in this situation, there isn't one.

After Mom has paid and called us a car, we sit in one of her favorite Italian restaurants off Wilshire. It's a cell phone free zone, which means I can slurp my pasta, and no one will post it on Instagram or Facebook later.

Mom's words from earlier have stayed with me. They're on replay in my mind, her voice soft in my ear. I'm waiting to tell Noah when I see him later. It's our last free week before the season starts.

I'm mid-bite when I put my fork down. "Earlier, someone asked about Quinn's girlfriend. What did he mean?" I look from Elle to our mom, who shrugs.

"Quinn doesn't have a girlfriend. He'd tell me," Mom says.

Elle chokes on her soda. "You're the last person he'd tell. He would tell Uncle Liam or Noah, first."

"Noah hasn't said anything to me," I add.

"He hasn't said anything to me, either," Elle says. "But a few weeks or so ago, Mom and I were at the coffee shop and this girl came up to him and said something about knowing his sister, which let's be real, even if she thought she knew you, she'd think I was you, ya know?"

I nod.

"Anyway, I've been in a few times, she's flirty with him. Dana even said she was hanging around their table the one time she went in to talk to him."

"Gotcha," I say. I'd like for Quinn to find someone, although not sure how she'd fair with this family of ours. It's a lot to take sometimes. I glance at our mom, she's completely lost in thought. "You okay, Mom?"

She looks up and smiles. "Just thinking about the first time we all met Quinn."

"Christmas with Liam, Josie, and Noah," Elle reminds us.

"The three of you were so small. I could hug all of you at the same time."

Elle and I both reach for her hand. "I'm sure you still can if you try. I'll call and beg Quinn to come out to the beach house this weekend," I tell her.

"I'd like that. Everyone will be there. Just like old times," she says before going back to her food.

The last thing my parents are is old, but with all of us growing up and doing our own thing, I imagine life is so different for them now.

NOAH

I never thought I'd feel relieved that Peyton found a dress. I know the bride's dress is an important part of a wedding, but in all honesty, I don't care if she's wearing shorts and a tee-shirt, I just want to marry her. Although, now that I think about it, if she were in my jersey, I'd really like that.

Of course, I broke a cardinal rule when I asked to see it. After she told me she fell in love with it the moment she stepped into it, I had to see what the fuss was all about. Huge no-no on my part, which doesn't make sense since she gets to see my suit and helped me pick it out. This wedding stuff is confusing.

Things with the Pioneers have settled down. I've been working my tail off to make sure the owners know where my heart is. It's in Portland. It's there that I want to buy a house and start a family with Peyton. The city, it's really amazing when it comes to their sports teams. The vibe is contagious, and it's where I want to be. Right in the heart of it.

While Peyton has been in Los Angeles doing wedding

stuff, I've been looking for houses. I've found a few that I like, one that overlooks the city. It's near to where I took Peyton a few weeks ago after I almost destroyed the single best thing that's ever happened to me. There are times when I get lost in my own head, forgetting that I have a partner. The crap the Rams pulled... I let that get the better of me and took it out on Peyton. If she hadn't shown up at practice, I don't know where my head would be right now.

Some of the guys gave me a lot of shit when Peyton was announced as staff. The ribbing can be fun for the most part, but I carry a certain amount of fear. Not that I don't think Peyton knows her shit, because she does. I just think the guys won't take her seriously because she's female. I hope she busts their balls so I can laugh at them.

As soon as my plane touches down, I text her.

Hey babe, just landed. Headed to the beach house.

Hurry! Quinn's bringing someone home. My mom says she walked in on them doing it.

Doing it?

IT

IT could be a lot of things.

S.E.X.

I know. I just wanted to hear you say it.

I didn't say anything. I typed it.

Smarty

Love you, HURRY!!!

I pocket my phone with a big smile on my face. It's been a week since I've seen her. She officially doesn't start her job until Monday, however, she's been watching game film each night, reporting back to the coaches on what needs to be worked on. I'm the only one privy to this information though, and I'm hoping that once she's on the sidelines, the guys will see that she knows what she's talking about.

The entire ride to the beach house, I'm tempted to phone Quinn to find out what's really going on. I'm having a tough time believing that Katelyn walked in on him unless he was at the beach when this all happened. Either way, whoever he's bringing to meet the gang better have some super thick skin. I love Elle, and of course Peyton, but damn those girls can be feisty and they are super protective of their brother.

Peyton is pacing out front when the car service drops me off. "What's wrong?" I ask as soon as she opens the car door.

"Nothing, can't I just be excited to see you?"

As soon as I'm out, I drop my carry-on and pull her into my arms. Soon, we'll see each other so much, she's liable to get sick of me. "Did you miss me?"

She nods and presses her lips to mine. "I always miss you."

"Me too." With my suitcase being towed behind me, Peyton and I walk toward her parents' house. "So, Quinn?"

"He didn't say anything when you went camping?"

"Not a word, but honestly babe, guys don't sit around and talk like you girls do. We discuss manly shit like beer, sports, and guns."

Peyton stops dead in her tracks and looks at me. "Guns? Noah Westbury, you don't own a gun. Do you even know how to shoot one?"

"Not the point."

"Doesn't matter. Don't make stuff up. Your manly

99

discussions are about burping, farting, and other gross bodily functions."

I start to laugh. She's not far from the truth. We do act a bit more relaxed when the women in our lives aren't around. "Seriously, babe. He never said anything."

She doesn't look like she believes me. Thing is, if Quinn had said something, I'm not sure I'd tell her. The guy doesn't stand a chance when it comes to women, especially in this family.

Out back, our entire family is gathered around the fire pit. Betty Paige runs up to me, launching herself into my arms. She's the best thing to have happened to our family. I hug her tightly before setting her back onto the ground. "You gonna be at my home opener?"

"Eh, I'm not sure football's really my thing anymore," she says so nonchalantly that I almost believe her. My mouth drops open and she giggles. "Of course, I am. Mom ordered me a bunch of new shirts and stuff for me to wear. Grandma Bianca and Grandma and Grandpa say they're going to be there too."

"A full house, I can't wait."

Paige and I walk over to the group. She goes back to her seat and picks up her phone. I hope she's playing a game, but something tells me she's texting Mack. I'm waiting for my parents to nip this budding relationship soon before something drastic happens. I kiss my mom, Katelyn, and Jenna on their cheeks; hug my dad, Harrison, and JD before grabbing a bottle of beer and taking a seat. Peyton and Elle have disappeared, leading me to believe they're out front, waiting for Quinn. I'm tempted to run interference, but the ambush is going to happen, regardless.

"Would you like something to eat?" my mom asks.

"Sure, if you're going in. I'll take something."

She rests her hand on my shoulder. "I'll be right back."

All around, the guys talk. It's mostly band stuff and I'm content to stare at the fire. The next time we're all together like this will be opening day if they can all come, and then the wedding.

"Noah, have you heard the demo from Elle's band?" Dad asks. I shake my head. He pulls out his phone and taps the screen a few times. Quinn's voice rings out. My head starts bobbing to the music. I like it. I knew he had talent, but he's really good. By the look on my dad's face, he agrees.

The clearing of a throat has us all looking toward the house. There's Quinn, holding hands with a very pretty woman.

"Quinn, didn't hear you come in," Harrison says. "This must be Nola." He stands and walks over to shake her hand and introduces himself. Quinn follows by introducing his girlfriend to the rest of us, and all I can think is that he got caught, like a horny teenager, having sex. I want to bust out laughing but don't want to embarrass my best friend.

"Where are Peyton and Elle?" Quinn asks.

I lean slightly and see the twins standing behind their brother. By the look of things, I'm guessing they went inside and had a pow-wow on how they were going to handle this newcomer, instead of waiting for their brother out front. Poor Nola. I wish I could give her some advice, but since I've been a part of the family forever, as has Ben since he moved to Beaumont, neither of us could possibly tell her anything useful. Ben slaps me in the arm and doesn't even try to hide his laughter. He knows all too well how dangerous Elle can be.

"Right behind you," I hear Elle say. Quinn turns slowly, his face showing so much fear. As tempted as I am to rib Quinn about this whole situation, I don't. I know my time's coming with Betty Paige, probably sooner than expected. My sister is infatuated with Mack, which to me isn't a good sign.

"How's the team shaping up?" Ben asks.

"It's good. Our rookies are going to make a difference and the offseason training the backs did is really showing. My arm is stronger too."

Ben nods toward Peyton. "Is she going to be a good fit?"

"Hell yes, she is. Even if it's only for my own benefit."

"I feel bad for Quinn."

"Me too. I was just thinking that you and I had it so easy."

"Mostly you." It's like Ben is reading my thoughts. "This girl doesn't stand a chance with those two."

"Or her." I point toward Eden who is running as fast as she can with her surfboard under her arm. This isn't going to be good. For a while, we've all thought Eden was harboring a crush on Quinn, but Jenna says it's purely a brother/sister type relationship because he surfs with her. By the look on her face, I'm going to go out on a limb and say it's definitely a crush.

"Shit, this day keeps getting better and better."

"We're like a damn soap opera," I mumble, watching as everything unfolds.

Whatever Quinn says to Eden sends her running toward the water with her surfboard. Quinn looks upset, but JD tells him not to worry. There's something about her knickers being twisted. Still after all these years, I have a hard time understanding JD's lingo.

Quinn brings Nola over to the fire and sits down. Instantly, band talk starts, which means I tune out. The music bug didn't really bite me as much as it did with Quinn. Maybe if I had grown up with it, things would be different. Mom often says I have the best parts of my dad. If I didn't know better, I would think that she's not a fan of *the* Liam Page, but I know that's not true.

"Nola, where are you from?" Peyton asks her. I reach for her hand and give it a squeeze. She's trying. More than Elle at the moment.

"I'm from South Carolina but spent the last four years in Idaho for college."

"Gamecocks fan?" Peyton asks.

Nola nods, and she and Peyton start discussing college football. I'm about to tune out until Nola calls the NFL the 'no fun league.' Of course, I'm in mid swallow and end up spraying beer all over the place. My dad starts laughing and Peyton's eyes go wide.

"Did I say something wrong?"

"Noah's the quarterback for the Portland Pioneers," Quinn tells her.

She covers her face from embarrassment. "Is there anyone in your family that isn't famous?"

Many hands go up. "Don't worry, sweetie. You'll get used to it," Katelyn says.

"Are you saying you had no idea who Quinn's family is?" Peyton asks.

Nola nods. "Up until the other day, I had no idea who Liam Page was."

Everyone in our circle busts out laughing, except for Nola. I can't imagine what's going through her mind right now, but sense that she'll have no problem fitting in with the rest of us. Still, she has a battle on her hands where Elle is concerned. I'm confident though that Peyton and Nola will get along just fine.

I excuse myself so I can go clean up. Peyton follows. She sits down on her bed and sighs. "What's wrong?"

"I'm not sure I like her."

"You just met her. Give her some time to find her groove. Our family is a tight nut to crack."

"It's not just that. There's something... odd. Like who doesn't know who your dad is?"

I shrug and pull a clean shirt out of my bag. "Maybe she listens to country music."

"I think you should go out without a shirt on."

I pause and rub my hand up and down my chest and abs. She smiles and beckons me with her finger. "Be careful Miss James, we're at your parents' house, and you know what that means."

"I know, but I haven't seen you in what feels like forever. I've missed you."

Leaning down, I kiss her nose. "We'll have to run some errands a bit later. Take a nice long drive somewhere."

Peyton pulls her lower lip in between her teeth and places her hands around my neck. "Do you promise?"

I start at the tip of her nose and kiss a path toward her ear. "I promise."

13

PEYTON

*A*s much as I love my parents, I hate staying here when I'm with Noah, especially after we haven't seen each other for a while. Noah's headstrong when it comes to respecting my parents. This is an admirable quality, but not one I wish to practice. And I'm certain my parents wouldn't care. Not that I'm going to ask them if they mind whether Noah and I have sex or not in their house, but I'm tempted.

Noah and I must've dozed off because voices jolt me awake. He's fast asleep and hugging me to his chest. Quinn's voice carries through the wall. He's taken Nola into his room. I can't really hear what they're saying, but much like I was in high school, I find myself wanting to sit against the wall with my ear pressed to it, listening. Elle and I used to get into so much trouble when a girl would call for him. We'd pick up the other line and make ridiculous sounds after she professed her undying love for him. Our dear brother started calling us the terror twins. Elle and I didn't mind. We never thought any of those girls were good enough for Quinn. It takes someone really special to match with our brother.

"Hey." I shake Noah slightly to wake him up. "I think Quinn and Nola are having sex."

"Doubt it," he mumbles.

"It's true. It's his new thing. He likes getting caught in awkward situations."

Noah rolls over, pinning me under his weight. Oddly, being like this is comforting. It's almost as if he's protecting me from the world. In a way, I know he is. When we're not together, we both feel off and just full of anxiety. Noah from not being able to hover over me, and me being afraid of my own shadow and needing him nearby. We should probably seek some sort of help, but I rather like that we're dependent on each other and I hope these feelings never go away.

"Maybe we should buy a house here."

Noah pushes himself up onto his elbows and looks at me. "We could, if you want. Do you want to live by your parents?"

"It would give us a lot of privacy when we're here."

"True. Owning multiple properties is a tax benefit."

"But an unneeded expense." The thought of wasting money on a piece of property scares me. "How long would we stay here?"

Noah looks to the wall for the answer. "Offseason. We can split our time between here and Beaumont."

"And in Beaumont, we can stay at my house."

"I don't think that's a good idea, Peyton. I love your parents, but let's be honest. I'd like to be with you whenever and not have to sneak off for long drives where we can get busted by the cops."

I laugh so hard, I snort. Before I can cover my mouth,

Noah kisses me. I wiggle my hips until he's situated between them, the ache and desire I feel for him growing rapidly. "How soon until we can buy a place?"

"Tomorrow." He barely breaks away to answer. Right now, it seems like it's going to be forever when in reality, it's hours away. Noah pulls away and rests his forehead to mine. Both of us are breathing heavily. I know that any minute from now, he's going to get up and leave me. Damn that respect he has.

Sure enough, he rolls off me and sits on the side of the bed, slightly bent at his waist. I reach for him, resting my hand on his side. He turns, looking at me from over his shoulder and smiles. "I'm going to call Allen and see if he knows a realtor down here, someone who is willing to work fast."

"Thank you."

"Anything for you." Noah starts to come toward me and pauses. I look at him questioningly as he turns his head slightly toward the wall Quinn and I share.

"What is it?"

"I think I just heard Quinn say something about surfing."

"Duh. As if Quinn isn't going to surf while he's here." I feel like I should roll my eyes at this point because Noah knows better.

"Do you care if I go out with him?"

I pretend to think for a minute. Let's see, my hot as hell fiancé, in a wet-suit. Yes, I'll take the visual any day of the week. Unless it's on Sunday and he's wearing his tight pants that make his ass look amazing. "I'll use the time to get to know Nola."

"I think Quinn would love that as I'm sure Elle is avoiding her."

I slip out of bed, braid my hair, and slip into my flip-flops. "Elle's just worried about her business. I would be too. She has a lot on her plate right now. She wants to succeed, and Quinn is a big part of that. And, she's trying to make sure his foray into the industry is a better experience than the one our dads had. We've all heard the horror stories. The last thing she wants to be is someone like Sam."

Noah doesn't say anything. I brought up a sore subject. Although I don't remember Sam, he does. He remembers the arguments his parents had about her and how much his mom worried when the band would go on tour.

"I'll see you there." I give him a quick kiss and make my way out of the room. As I pass by Quinn's, I notice the door is open. From the living room, I can see a faint outline of our family outside and off to the side is a sole person. Nola, I'm assuming. That's where I head.

About five steps into the sand, I'm kicking off my flip-flops. Turning to the left and then right, I realize that I do want to live here. Maybe not right next to my parents, but somewhere along this stretch of beach. It's what I know, and it's where Noah told me that he'd fight for us.

The benefit of walking in sand is that you can sneak up on people. I don't know what I expected to find when I stood behind her. Maybe her texting someone about our family or looking at her phone instead of watching my brother and Eden surf. I hate that I thought negatively about her because she's laughing each time Quinn crashes and gasping when Eden catches a wave and rides it flawlessly.

As soon as Noah runs by, I must choose. Either I sit down or walk away. "He's been doing this since he could walk." I decide to take the spot next to Nola. "You should go out there, Quinn's a good teacher. He taught us."

"I think I'm okay being a spectator. How come you're not out there?"

I don't tell her that sometimes my leg hurts and that the only thing I want to do is sit. Or that I'm afraid my leg might give out while I'm standing on the board. Not that I haven't fallen before, but falling when I'm out there, with the guys around me, would be a circus. What I do tell her is that I'd like to get to know her better and that Quinn must think she's the one if he brought her into our madhouse. Because that's what we are, a highly functioning blended madhouse of a family.

"We haven't known each other long."

Of course they haven't. However, it's been long enough that some paparazzi picked up on the fact that they're spending time together. I wonder if she knows, and I wonder if they've made Page Six or some other gossip magazine out there. It's been years since I looked at those sites, not since Noah and I finally got together.

"My brother doesn't do things hastily. That's Elle. She's the jump first, ask questions later. I'm the planner in the family. I have a plan for everything, except my wedding but that's another story for another day." I purposely leave out that a date's set, I have my dream dress, and my flowers are on order. While I think Quinn is serious about her, I'd hate for her to assume she would be his plus one. "Quinn? He's the one who sits on the sidelines and makes sure everyone's taken care of, never worrying about himself. It's nice to see him with his guard down. Like I said, you must be it for him."

Nola and I both stare out at the surf, watching Eden,

Quinn, and Noah wait until a wave big enough starts to form.

"I'm not sure I believe in love at first sight," she says.

"I do. I've been in love with him for as long as I can remember, before I even knew what love was, I knew I was going to marry him."

"When was that?"

I laugh because it's so absurd to think I fell in love with Noah while in kindergarten. "Oh, when I was about five or so."

"Oh, wow."

"Yeah, it took us a long time to figure things out, plus there's an age difference. I'm fairly sure my parents would've killed Noah if we started dating when I was fifteen or sixteen."

"How far apart are you?"

"Five years, but when you're young, age matters."

"Yeah, I suppose it does. When's your wedding?" I give her the song and dance about wanting a winter wedding and tell her Noah wants a summer one. Truth is, Noah would get married right this second if I yelled out to him that it had to be now. He doesn't care about the formalities, just that we're going to be husband and wife. I explain the issue with his schedule, and now mine and tell her why a winter wedding won't work. I should tell her the truth, but I don't want to put Quinn into a situation he may not be ready for. Although, I can't imagine he wouldn't bring her if they're together.

"Why not just elope?"

I pull my legs to my chest and instantly feel her eyes on me. It's too late to hide my scar or to run away. The only thing I can do is ignore her penetrating gaze. "We've been through a lot, or I have, and I want the fairy tale."

"Quinn said you were in an accident."

Nola looks like she's been caught with her hand in the cookie jar, but it's the opposite. "Yeah, you're definitely the one. Quinn doesn't talk about much of anything to people outside our family so if he told you, he must trust you."

She looks away immediately and I sense that she's hiding something. I want to ask her what's on her mind, but I don't want to be nosy. We sit in silence until Mom approaches us.

"Peyton, do you think I could have a minute with Nola?"

As soon as I stand, my mom gives me a hug. "Be nice to her," I whisper in her ear. Mama bear is about to come out, I can see it in her face. She tries to smile, but it barely moves her lips. She has always been protective over Quinn because of what his biological mom did to him, and now that he's brought someone home, well I have a feeling my mom is about to show a side of her that rarely comes out.

"Love you, sweetie," she replies before letting me go.

I take a few steps away before looking back. My mom's face is expressionless, her lips are moving, but I can't hear anything. She's keeping her voice down and by the look on Nola's face, my mother is laying down the law. Poor Quinn. If it's not Elle and I always up in his business, making his life crazy with sisterly drama, it's our mother. She's a hen most of the time, but damn if her claws aren't out right now giving this poor unsuspecting girl the rules of dating her son.

14

NOAH

*P*eyton and I drive up and down the coastline. Her arm is hanging out of the window and her long ponytail is blowing in the breeze. I figured if we are staying in L.A. until training camp starts, we might as well take advantage of the beautiful weather and rent a convertible. Honestly, I am a bit shocked that Peyton agreed. There's still some hesitation when it comes to getting into cars, which I try to accommodate with full-size SUVs.

Up ahead, the real estate agent Allen suggested we hire, signals that she's about to make a turn. I feel bad for her, having to deal with us. We're excited, eager, and very particular about what we want. The house must have a view, beach access and a pool. We've seen half a dozen so far, but none of them are what we're looking for.

We pull up along the curb and the first thing I notice is there isn't a gate. Well there is, but it's more like a fence. There's no privacy from the onlookers. I'm not sure I like that. Peyton and I look at the house. With the trees in the front, it's hard to see, but honestly, I'm not feeling it. "I think this is going to be a no for me."

"Me too," she says. "I can't smell the ocean." Peyton and I get out of the car and meet Phyllis as she's rushing toward us. She opens the small gate, which we could've easily stepped over and waited for us to pass by.

"This home is new within the last two years. It has eight bedrooms and bathrooms and is eight thousand square feet. Now it's a little different than what I've shown you already, but I believe it has everything you're looking for."

While she continues to talk, Peyton and I look at each other. We're not superstitious, but certain things stick out, like the number eight. We rush to get out of the car and follow our agent up the cobblestone steps.

"This home has a traditional New England feel. The builder added cedar shingles and..." She opens the front door and has us step inside. "This is something fun." We watch as she unlatches and opens the top half of the door.

"That's neat," Peyton says. She's skeptical, I can see it in her features.

"Yes, it gives the house character. Now if you'll step inside, this is what we call an open-air living home."

Peyton and I step into the living room and stand there. I don't know about her, but my mouth is hanging open. The sheer beauty of what I'm looking at, aside from my fiancée, is unbelievable.

"There are numerous sets of pocket doors that slide away, giving you open indoor living areas to the loggia, terraces, the courtyard and main patio where the pool is located. Throughout the main floor, there are skylights to bring in more natural light, vaulted ceilings, and tongue and groove flooring. All the rooms have walk-in closets.

The great room has a fireplace, the kitchen is state of the art, and downstairs you'll find a lounge with a pub bar and wine cellar. As well as a home theater."

I can hear Phyllis talking, but the words don't make sense. I'm stuck on the view and the curtains blowing from the light breeze. Peyton and I stand next to each other, overlooking the patio below and the ocean. We may not have direct beach access, but there's a wooden walkway leading to the beach.

"The beach access is shared by the houses on each side of you," Phyllis says as if reading our minds.

Reluctantly, we have to finish the tour of the home. Phyllis takes us by an elevator to the basement showing us the six-car underground garage. I don't even have two cars, let alone six. As I stand there, looking at the pristine concrete, I see myself throwing a football with my son or daughter. I see my children driving those hot wheel motorized cars. I see a happy life developing. The next floor is nothing but entertainment. The wine cellar, home theater, swimming pool and outside shower. Everything we want, with a few things we hadn't even considered.

"Sunsets from this patio are going to be amazing," Peyton says as we stand outside. She's right. Three Adirondack chairs sit perfectly on this small patch of turf, facing the ocean. I can easily see Peyton and I out here, each night, holding hands as the sun goes down. It's her words that spur me to do the most irrational thing ever.

"We'll take it," I say to Phyllis, who just nods. Selling multi-million-dollar homes is her job, nothing fazes her.

"Noah, we haven't even looked at the rest of the house."

I kiss Peyton on the tip of her nose. "We don't need to. We're already in love with this house. I can see us living here, having our family over. Most importantly, I can see us raising a family within these walls. The minute we stepped into the living room and saw the view, I knew you'd want to live here. It's like your parents' condo. The only drawback is that the beach is yards away, not inches, but the view makes up for it. We'd wake up to this every morning and go to sleep with the sound of waves crashing not far from us."

"I agree, Noah." She rises and kisses me hard. "We're buying a house."

We are, and it feels right.

"I still want to see the rest of the house," she says to Phyllis, who motions us to follow her.

Bedroom after bedroom, and bathroom after bathroom, we tour our new home. Phyllis is on the phone, yammering about closing the deal, while Peyton and I walk in and out of closets, sit in bathtubs, and marvel at not one but two kitchens, plus a massive laundry room.

"I think Thanksgiving, will be here this year."

I push down on the countertop in the kitchen and then tug it. "I think we should spend a week christening each room."

Peyton slaps my chest. "We'll need longer than a week."

I pull her into my arms. "We're really doing this."

She nods against my chest and tightens her arms around my waist. "This seems like such a bigger deal than getting married."

Her words sink in. She's right, it does. "There isn't anything that I don't want to do with you, Peyton."

"I feel the same way."

"Sorry to interrupt, but my colleague informed me that there's already an offer on the home. It came in about an hour ago," Phyllis sighs. "They also offered above asking price."

Peyton's expression falls, but mine doesn't. I shrug. "We'll pay cash and we'll offer a million over."

"Noah," Peyton exclaims.

"What? Might as well put my trust fund to good use."

"I'll pay half. I want to."

I glance at Phyllis and motion for her to let her colleague know this house is off the market. This is where the next generation of Westbury's is going to start, and there isn't anyone or anything that can stand in our way.

THE DOWNSIDE TO BUYING A HOUSE – the paperwork. I thought offering cash would be simple. But no, sign here, dot there, put your blood stamp here. By the time hour four came around, I found myself ordering food from a delivery service because I was starving. Peyton gave me a wicked side eye but had no qualms about helping herself to the greasy bag of burgers that I ordered. I have no shame when I'm hungry.

The benefits of paying with cash and being a celebrity is that the banks want to accommodate us. Once the owners accepted our offer, Phyllis started our paperwork and our lawyer busted his ass making sure everything's in order and that the house is in perfect condition. Not that I expected the house to have any issues.

Peyton and I arrive at her parents to retrieve our bags. It would make sense for us to spend one more night here because it's getting late, but the thought of waking up in our new home is far too appealing. We bought the house completely furnished, which will save us time and a fortune from having to refurbish. The linens have to change, but Peyton and I can do that tomorrow.

"I think tonight, we sleep out under the stars."

"There are four beds in the house, we can't find a usable one?"

"Eh," I say as I shut off the car. "I take that back. Sleep is not in the cards for us tonight. Naps only."

"Naps?"

I want to pull her across the console and show her what I mean, but the yelling coming from her parents' house is alarming. "Stay here." I get out, slam the car door and rush toward the condo. The door flings open and Katelyn is barreling toward me.

"I'll kill her," she yells, causing me to stop dead in my tracks.

"She's my fucking problem. I'll take care of it," Harrison says. We don't make eye contact as he chases down Katelyn. He reaches for her arm, pulling her to him. "Goddamn it, Katelyn. Stop."

"I will not. She's gone too far."

"I'll take care of it, Katelyn. I don't fucking trust her. I don't want her to hurt you."

I don't know what's going on, but things don't look good. In the brief moment of silence, I hear the car door slam and before I can intervene, Peyton is rushing around the corner, yelling about Alicia being in town at the Bean Song.

"I need to go to my son," Katelyn says. "He needs me. He needs to know that *I'm* his mom no matter what."

"I'll drive you," I blurt out, but Peyton shakes her head.

"No, I'll go with my mom. Please stay with my dad and make sure he doesn't do anything irrational."

"Stay out of this, Peyton," Harrison admonishes.

"Why? You don't think I know how you feel about her? Or how Quinn feels? Or Mom? You don't think I haven't read the book Sam wrote? This is our life, Dad. For as long as I can remember that woman has lingered in the background, making my brother feel like he didn't deserve to be loved. For years, Quinn lived in fear that she was going to come in the middle of the night and take him away. We may not share blood, but we're his family and he needs us. He needs Mom, Elle, and me. He needs to know we're his family and we'll do anything to protect him."

"Alicia..." Harrison sighs. "I'm afraid she's dangerous. You don't know her. You don't know what she's capable of. I don't know what the fuck I would do if something were to happen to you, your mom or sister." He grabs at his beanie and growls. "Fuck. Fuck this shit. I'm going to fucking kill her."

"Well, hell hath no fury like a pissed off mother," Katelyn says angrily. I feel like I need to yell out booyah or give her a nice pat on the back for being a fierce bitch.

Peyton walks over to me and collapses in my arms. "I got you," I tell her as she starts to weep. "I'll come with you."

"I'll be fine. I'll call you and let you know what's going on. I'm sorry."

I pull away and cup her cheeks. "You never have to apologize for wanting to protect your family, Peyton. Our house, it's not going anywhere, and we still have a few weeks until we have to be back in Portland. Go. Go take care of your brother and let him know I'm here when and if he wants to talk." I kiss her quickly and nudge her toward her mother, who is waiting at the end of the walkway. I go over and stand next to Harrison and watch as they pull out of the driveway.

"Most of my life is in that car."

"Mine too," I tell him. "Do you need me to call my dad or anything?"

Harrison shakes his head. "No, I'm going to follow them. I need to speak to Quinn and figure out where Alicia is, and end this once and for all." Harrison heads toward the garage and within seconds his motorcycle roars to life.

I'm left standing there, wondering what the hell I should do besides pace. After phoning my parents, pacing is exactly what I end up doing, checking my phone every few minutes for Peyton's call.

15

PEYTON

*M*y mom speeds down the freeway, weaving in and out of traffic. Her hand is glued to the horn, yet no one seems to care. I have one hand on the door handle and the other is clutching my seat. This could be reminiscent of the accident I was in, but Kyle wasn't being a daredevil and trying to kill us. Not that my mom is either but tell my mother the one thing she doesn't want to hear, and she becomes a madwoman.

When the text came in from my sister, I thought it was a joke. The words "Alicia's back" could've meant anything but to our family it means the depths of hell have risen, and to my mom, it means her son's in trouble. And that's how I find myself sitting in the passenger seat, while my cool, calm, and normally collected mom curses at every car that gets in her way.

She finally exits, but the onslaught of dangerous driving continues. I don't know why I said I would come with her. Maybe because it's my brother and he needs all of us around, or maybe it's because I didn't want my mom to be alone with her thoughts. There will be no eyewitness to give an account of the brutality my mother will enforce on that wretched monster, and I'll happily help dispose of her body.

We're close to Quinn's when I hear her sob. I look over and see her staring toward my side of the car. My mom pulls over and pushes the button to drop my window down. "Quinn!"

The man turns. It's my brother and my heart breaks. I open the door and rush to him, wrapping my arms tight around his waist. "Quinn, I'm sorry."

He doesn't say anything. There doesn't need to be words to match his sobs. I'm pushed away, replaced by my mother. Anyone else would be jealous, but I'm not. He needs her. He always has. They share a bond like no other.

"My son," she says as she holds his face. "Get in the car, honey."

He does, crawling into the backseat. I follow, sliding in next to him. Quinn lets me hold his hand. He doesn't talk and only stares out the window. When we arrive at his apartment, my mom doesn't shut off the car.

"Peyton, I need some time alone with Quinn."

I nod in understanding and start to slide out of the car. Quinn's hand grabs ahold of my wrist, halting my exit.

"She's going to come to the apartment. She has a bag of clothes on my bed, give them back to her and tell her I don't want to ever see her again."

"Alicia?" I hate saying her name aloud and cringe at the look on my brother's face.

He shakes his head. "Nola. I'm through with her. Done. What she did, it's unforgivable."

"What has she done?"

He doesn't say anything.

"Quinn," I say his name softly. "Maybe you should talk to her."

He looks at me. His eyes are bloodshot, and his face is blotchy. I can't remember the last time I saw him like this, if ever. He may be a somber guy, but never overly emotional. "She played me, P. She brought that woman into my life, blindsided me in a place where I felt safe. I'm done. She lied about who she is and what she's doing here, all because of who she knows. I can't have people like that in my life. People associated with—"

"Okay," I tell my brother, holding my hands up. "Okay." I don't need to hear any more. The girl he brought home to meet us has betrayed him in the worst way. Quinn can take a lot, but not when it comes to the woman who abandoned him.

My mom drives away with Quinn. I stand there in the parking lot, watching the red taillights of her SUV until they've blended in with the other cars on the road. Inside, his apartment is clean, and it smells girly. You can easily tell a woman's touch has been here.

I find the bag Quinn told me about and set it by the door. Part of me is hoping she doesn't show up here, but if this were me, I would. I'd knock and pound on that door, demanding he listen to me. Although, I ran from Noah when things got hairy between us. I shut down and acted like I was fine, but I wasn't. I was cut deep, bleeding from the stab wounds inflicted by him and Dessie. He'll never know though because telling him only hurts him and I love him far too much to do that.

My phone rings and his beautiful face fills my screen. I smile, despite the situation. "Hello, handsome."

"Hey, babe," he says. "My dad just got here. How's Quinn?"

"There's been an issue."

"Are you okay?" I'm always his first concern no matter what.

"I'm fine. I'm at Quinn's. It seems that..." I take a deep breath and close my eyes for a moment. "Nola had something to do with Alicia being here."

The silence is deafening until Liam lets out a roar of some sort. "Noah?"

"I'm here, Harrison just called and spoke to my dad."

"This is bad," I say.

"Very much. Where's Quinn?"

I shake my head, even though he can't see me. "I don't know. My mom took him somewhere to talk."

"I'm coming to you, Peyton. Sit tight and try not to worry. I knew I shouldn't have let you leave with your mom."

At Noah's words, tears slip from my eyes. "It's hard, Noah. I love my brother so much and I've never seen him like this. He's hurting."

"Everything will be okay, I promise. I love you, P. I'll be there shortly."

"I love you, please hurry. I don't want to be alone."

It turns out that I'm not alone. As soon as we hang up, there's pounding on the door, followed by some yelling. If I hadn't been expecting Nola to show up, I'd be scared out of my mind right now.

"Quinn, open up. We need to talk. Please, Quinn."

I open the door and stare down Nola, with a tear-streaked face. I want to rage. I want to grab her by the neck and ask her what the hell she was thinking. Instead,

I hold onto the doorknob, squeezing it until the pain sets in.

"Elle—" she says. The need to roll my eyes is great. I refrain. It's a common mistake but one that is making things worse for Nola at the moment.

"It's Peyton."

"Oh, the nice one." I tilt my head to the side as if I'm asking her if she really just said something so rude. She closes her eyes and wipes angrily at her face. "I'm sorry, that was incredibly rude of me."

Instead of placating her, I tell her how things are in my family. "Listen, when it comes to my family, I'm as wicked as the next person. My brother, he doesn't want to see you. In fact..." I reach down and hand her the bag of clothes. "I believe these are yours. He says you don't have a key, so I don't need to ask for that back. I suggest you run along back to the Tuckers because you're not wanted here."

"Wait, please?"

I sigh, and this time I do roll my eyes.

"Please tell Quinn that I love him. All I lied about was my name and who I was, not because I was hiding anything from him, it was because I was hiding from myself. I can't explain Sofia and Alicia, other than I went to school with Sofia and we were roommates and I thought best friends. She talked about him all the time."

"So, you knew who he was?" I cross my arms over my chest. "You knew who my entire family was and pretended like you didn't."

"Yes and no."

"It can't be both."

"Yes, I know, but Sofia—"

"What is she doing here?"

Elle stands behind Nola, the murderous rage in her eyes is something I've never seen before. Not only did Nola mess with our brother, but she's screwing around with one of Elle's musicians, and that group is so important to my sister.

Nola steps back as Elle stalks toward her until she's pinned against the wall. I should intervene, but I don't.

"I'm only going to tell you once, get the hell out of here. Don't you ever call my brother again and don't even think about showing up here. You've done so much damage, you have no idea. You have no clue what you've done, bringing that wretched woman into his life. I want you gone. I don't ever want to see or hear from you again. And for the love of all things holy, you better hope you're not pregnant because I'll make damn sure my brother takes that baby from you. You're not any better than the whore that gave him up. Now get out!"

My eyes drop open as Elle unleashes. She said everything I was thinking but would've never been able to put into words. Nola cries out and rushes down the stairs. Elle stands here, waiting until she can no longer see her. When she turns to face me, the angry sister is gone, and tears are now in her eyes.

We fall into each other's arms and cry. We've always known Alicia would come back again, but as the years went by, we expected it less. When Quinn turned eighteen, we walked around on eggshells for a year, waiting for word that she reached out to him. When he moved to California, I thought my mom was going to have a heart attack. She spent more time traveling back and forth between here and Beaumont. It felt like she lived on the airplane.

And it hurt Elle and me. Our mom was so focused on

Quinn, she missed things, but we understood. Growing up, he questioned everything. Mostly, why his mother couldn't love him the same way our mom loved him.

Elle and I are still standing in the doorway when Noah and Ben come rushing up the stairs. We break and go to our respective men, and both sob. The guys manage to get us back into the apartment, where the only thing we can do is wait. I text Quinn to let him know that he left just in time. I don't want to know or even think about what a confrontation between the two of them would be like right now.

We're anxious. The four of us. Ben had food delivered and Noah makes sure our phones stay charged in case someone tries to call. Elle paces while I stand and look out of the window, waiting for Quinn to come home.

"That bitch is going to fuck up my band," Elle seethes. Ben is by her side before I can respond. Quinn's stronger than the drama that surrounds him, at least I hope he is.

"We'll make sure Quinn has the support he needs," Noah says. I smile softly at him, silently thanking him. My brother is going to be Noah's best man, there isn't anything Noah won't do for his best friend.

"It's going to take Quinn a long time to recover from this. To trust anyone."

"Noah and I will take him out, get him shitty ass drunk and find him a one-night stand to help him get over this." Elle goes over to Ben and slaps him across his chest. "Ouch," he says.

"There will be more of that if you turn my brother into a man-whore. He needs friends and family. He needs to know that not all women are evil. He needs the band

and music. It's his passion, it's what he loves." My sister runs her hand through her hair and sighs.

She's right, but our brother loves Nola, and the pain she's caused, coupled with Alicia making her presence known isn't going to go away anytime soon.

16

NOAH

*I*t's opening day and I'm standing in the middle of the field, watching as fans walk toward their seats with hotdogs, nachos, candy, beer, and of course their favorite noise maker. The thing that always gets me is the foam finger. I never know if the fan is telling me I'm number one or if they're flipping me off. Last year, it was probably a little bit of both. But this year, the season is going to be different. Not only am I putting in every effort I can muster, but the team wants to win. No more subpar seasons for us. We want to make the playoffs, be a team that challenges every opponent. We want teams to have to earn their victory, and not come into our stadium thinking the game is a wash.

A few of my teammates are out on the field. Julius is running the snake as his warm-up. Right now, he's doing high knees, and almost kicking himself in the face. He asked if I wanted to do it with him. I thought he was joking at first, but his expression turned to stone when I laughed and had to politely decline.

At the fifty-yard line section of the stadium, behind

the team bench, I have half of the section reserved. I think every member of my family will be in attendance today. The last time this happened, I was a rookie. I wish I could say I'm the reason they're here, but it's not. It's Peyton. She's on the sideline, with her headset on and thumbing through a notebook. I've seen what's in there, copiously detailed notes about every Pioneer player. Even the third string guys.

The best part about today – we're playing the Rams. I have a strong desire to annihilate this team, not only for me but for Peyton as well – my girl spent hours studying game film on them and has shown us their weaknesses.

Actually, the best part about football right now is that the guys have really taken to Peyton. They listen to her, ask her questions when things aren't going their way, and respect her knowledge of the game. A few of the guys have told me that I better "wife her up" before they put the moves on her. I guess having a wedding date isn't good enough for them. I was never worried about the team accepting her. What scared me was whether or not she'd allow herself to fit in and express herself. She's never had a problem telling me where my game is weak, but telling others is a different story.

After training camp started, Peyton and I made a rule – don't bring work home. At the stadium or practice facility, she's a part of the coaching staff. At home, I'm the boss. Not really, but it's fun to say sometimes. We are equals. We're two people madly in love with each other, who are trying to plan a wedding while working crazy hours.

I finally get why she was so hesitant to set a date – the planning. Over the summer, everything was easier because we had the time. Once football started, time became almost non-existent. Her days are much longer than mine. She's spent hours watching game film, creating player profiles to her liking, and meeting with players and coaching staff. On top of this, she has to attend meetings, which she tells me is totally not her thing.

I've tried to help where I can. By help, I mean I called both moms and asked them to do the unthinkable and plan the rest of the wedding. I spent days photocopying the winter section of her wedding bible to send to our mothers. I've also made the guest list, inviting everyone we know. As for the wedding party, we decided to keep things small, which is surprising since Peyton was part of a sorority. I thought for sure we were going to have eight to ten people standing next to us, but she only wants our sisters. Telling Alex that he wasn't going to be in the wedding was a bit daunting. He's a big dude and could easily crush me if he wanted. Thankfully, he was cool and said he doesn't really look good in brown and would be there happily if an invitation found its way into his mailbox. Honestly, we're not expecting many people to come. Our families will be there for sure, but being as the wedding is Christmas night, we don't want to take people away from their families.

Two security guards are now standing on each side of the section I reserved. In the past, there would be one with a second lingering. However, Quinn will be here today and with Sinful Distraction's first album reaching number one on the charts, he's developed a fan base, and at one of our preseason games in California, it was a nightmare for him. Not to mention Nola. She's received a few death threats, which has Quinn on edge. He's so laid back that when he saw them on social media, he had a massive panic attack and wanted to hire round the clock security for her. It took my mom, his mom and Jenna to explain that sadly, this is normal and until someone physically sends Nola something or accosts her on the streets, they should ignore what they read. Still, I'd probably do the same thing as Quinn if I were in his shoes.

After Quinn flew to South Carolina to win back Eleanora, they've been stronger than ever. They're cute, according to Peyton, and she really likes having Nola around. Quinn and Nola are living together. It took a lot of prodding on everyone's part, but he finally dug into his trust fund and bought a house. Of course, it's on the beach, which shouldn't surprise anyone, and is close to Elle and Ben's house. Elle and Nola are cordial. Peyton is a bit more accepting of Nola. But I think in due time, everyone will put aside the small hiccup and things will be fine. I like Nola a lot. She makes my best friend happy and has brought him out of his shell a little bit. And I like her parents and brother Rhett, who will be at the game today as well.

I'm proud of Elle and everything's she accomplished with Sinful Distraction. She had this vision, and the drive to make sure the group succeeded. They're going to go on tour with 4225 West after the wedding. My dad, Harrison, and JD are very excited to be their opening act, which is unheard of. But they're family, and there isn't anything the band wouldn't do to help others out.

Peyton looks out toward the field, almost as if she knows I'm thinking about her. I want nothing more than to go over to her right now and kiss her, but not while we're at work. That's another rule. It's not one I want to follow but know I have to. My fantasy of having sex with her in the locker room can only play out in my mind. I get it, but it doesn't mean I like it. If players see us together, it can create a disconnect between her and the others. Here, we're player and coach. We try not to interact unless she's pointing something out or has a question for me.

Glancing back toward the stands, my dad, mom, grandparents, and sister are making their way down to their seats. I start to head over so I can talk to them when I notice my grandma Bianca. She's dressed head to toe in Pioneer gear, but that's not what catches my eye. It's the fact that her face is painted purple. She is, without a doubt, my biggest fan. I know she's making up for lost time, and I appreciate it, but she doesn't have to go to extremes like this. I'm sure the paint is uncomfortable.

As I pass by Peyton, our eyes meet. I wink, and she blushes. I may not be able to touch her right now, but I'm sure as hell going to flirt with her. We keep eye contact until I'm forced to look away.

Betty Paige is at the railing and starting to climb over by the time I get there. A stadium security guard yells something, but she ignores him. She jumps into my arms and clings as tightly as she can to my shoulders. There's going to be a day when I'm no longer her number one guy. It's a day that I'm not looking forward to.

"Everything okay?" I ask her. School has started for her, and Mack has a girlfriend. I knew that wasn't going to sit well with her when it happened, but it's for the best. When Nick called to tell me, my heart plummeted. Sometime over the summer, a girl a year or so older, took an interest in Mack, and I guess he really liked the attention. He effectively broke Paige's heart, which in a roundabout way makes my dad very happy.

"I'm getting better."

Teenage love. I don't recommend it and know that someday I'll be the dad nursing broken hearts. "He's just a boy, Betty Paige. And as much as it kills me to say this, there are so many other guys out there. Plus, you're way too young to settle down."

"But I love him."

Thankfully she can't see me roll my eyes. I don't discount that what she feels is love, but she's going to love many people throughout her years. She just doesn't understand that yet.

"If it's meant to be, it'll happen. You have to be patient."

"Like you and Peyton?"

"Yep. And Mom and Dad. We all had to wait."

"Being a teen sucks."

So does being an adult, but that's life. I set her down so I can help her get back over the wall. My dad is there to make sure she doesn't hurt herself.

"Is she nervous?" Dad asks, nodding toward Peyton. I look over my shoulder to find her head slightly bent toward her binder. No doubt, studying.

"I don't think so. I know she wants to beat the Rams pretty badly though."

"Can you blame her?"

"Not one bit. I'm going to do everything I can to make sure it happens, and so are the guys. They're pissed."

Dad pats me on my shoulder pad. "I don't blame them. It was shady what they did."

Shady doesn't begin to describe what the Rams did. Underhanded, deplorable. I feel as if they should've been fined by the league for their actions.

"Hey Grandma, looking good," I yell up to her. She stands and takes a bow. On the outside, she looks like a frail old lady, but her mind is sharp. Years of alcohol abuse are starting to show, and her health is declining. My dad doesn't say much about it, but I know he's hurting. They've been trying to make up for lost time.

Quinn is walking down the steps, flanked by security. There's a group of young girls following, yelling his name, and asking for his autograph. Nola's with him, holding onto his hand. By the looks of things, he's not going to get any peace being here. I look around for our marketing team members and call one of them over to me.

"Any way I can get two media passes for my friend?" I nod toward the stand where more security has shown up to try and get the girls back to their seats.

"Don't you have a booth?" Bobbie asks.

"I do, but it's the first game and they like to sit in the stands."

She steps away and pulls out her walkie-talkie. I don't want Quinn to leave but know he will if he doesn't feel comfortable. Bobbie comes back and hands me her clipboard. "Put their names here and go ahead and bring them down. I'll get their passes."

"Thank you." As soon as she walks away, I'm back at the railing. "Quinn!" I motion for him to follow me toward the gate.

"What's up?"

Security opens the metal door for us. "Come with me." They follow me back toward the bench, where they can stand for the game. "You'll be able to enjoy the game from here."

"Seriously?" Nola asks.

"Yeah, stay behind this line. There will be a waitress who will come around to see if you want anything to eat or drink. And Bobbie will be by with your passes, which allows you to stay on the field and have access to the clubhouse."

"Thanks, man." Quinn and I hug it out. I know he'll be more comfortable down here.

"Westbury?"

Ah, the sweet sound of my girl calling my name. "Yes, Miss James," I say when I get to her.

"What's that all about?" she asks, tilting her head toward her brother.

"The fans are out in droves. I thought he'd be at ease down here where no one can get to him."

Peyton eyes her brother and his girlfriend for a long minute. "You did that for him?"

"Yeah, why?"

"You've never done that for your dad."

I shrug. "Dad's had a much longer time to get used to the attention. This is all new to Quinn and I want him to enjoy the game."

Peyton looks at me, she smiles so brightly that my knees go weak. "You're really something, Noah Westbury."

Fuck it. I don't care who's looking or where we are right now. When my girl gives me a compliment like that, I'm going to kiss the shit out of her. And I do, right there in front of everyone. People behind us, mostly our family, cheer loudly. When we part, she looks at me with hooded eyes.

"Noah..."

"Don't worry, babe. I'll finish when we get home."

"Only if you win this game, Westbury."

"Consider the victory in the bag." I wink again and painstakingly walk away from her to join my team in warm-ups.

17

PEYTON

I have never been one to gloat or brag about my success or even Noah's when the time isn't right. It's a trait that I learned from my dad. He never talked about a hit that the band would have or comment on a song nominated for a Grammy until the time was right. That time being on the red carpet or during an interview. If someone came up to him in a grocery store and said something, my dad simply replied with a thank you.

Right now, I want to forget the lesson he taught me. I want to stand on my desk, dance a little jig, and run up and down the halls of the building, yelling about the headline in the paper. *James Makes a Difference.* Even without reading the article, I know it's about me.

When the reporter called and asked me a few questions, I had no idea what the article was going to be about, until last night when he emailed it to me, saying it would be on the front page of the paper. Not just local, but nationwide.

The picture of me is one taken from a recent game.

Julius Cunningham, Chase Montgomery, and I are talking about one of the plays. I don't remember exactly what I was saying, but in the picture, both guys are focused on what I'm telling them.

Taking this job, I was apprehensive. I didn't know how I'd fit in, whether they'd treat me as a coach, or if the guys would even listen to me. I also had reservations. There was a tiny voice in the back of my head that wouldn't go away. It kept reminding me that Noah's the quarterback and that he's the only reason I got the job. I think I've proven otherwise.

The Pioneers are eight and three going into the Thanksgiving holiday. They are off to their best start ever, which isn't saying much since they're an expansion team and only a few years old. However, this is where the owners saw their team all along, as one of the top contenders in the division, and I'm being credited with some of their success.

I say some because I can only do so much. The players, the guys who bust ass day in and day out, who put it all on the line any given Sunday deserve most, if not all, of the credit. They're winning because they're playing as a team. There isn't a single selfish player on the field who is looking to pad their stats. No one is looking to be a hero. Not even Noah, who is having a remarkable year. His trajectory is deadly, and the receivers are racking up yards by the hundreds to prove it. Our defensive line is holding offensives to an average of about twenty points per game, while our offense is scoring almost thirty a game. Not the best in the league, but better than anything they've done in the past.

"Knock, knock."

I look up from the article to find Logan Baker

standing in my doorway. My office has become my sanctuary. My parents bought me a painting for my wall. It's still sitting in the corner and will probably stay there. The weekend before training camp started, Noah and I came in and painted the walls with dry erase paint. I wanted to be able to utilize every inch with plays and notes, without cluttering my office. Right now, it looks like the playbook threw up all over the place with x's, o's and lines going in every which direction. Everyone knows if I'm not in here, you'll find me in the film room or on the field. I stay as far away from the players as possible, especially Noah. I don't want to give anyone an excuse to complain about either of us.

"Hey." Logan walks in and sits down in the chair in front of my desk. My secretary insisted that I have a chair in my office even though I rarely have anyone in here. Because I work mostly with the team, I meet with them on the field or in a classroom.

Over the past couple of months, Logan and I have become friends. He's young, ambitious, and wants to succeed. He bought this team with his inheritance and has put his blood, sweat, and tears into building a franchise.

"Great article," he says.

"It's..."

"You know, Peyton. It's okay to take credit for something you deserve."

"I can only show the guys what I see and give them suggestions on how to make a change. I can't physically go out there and play the game. That's on the players, the team."

Logan chuckles. I'm not sure what he finds funny about the whole situation. The last time I checked, football is a team sport, and you need eleven players doing their job, in hopes to score.

"Westbury tells me that you can throw the ball."

I scoff. Noah exaggerates everything when it comes to me. Lately, it's been my cooking. Sure, I can make the basics, but anything major and I'm calling for delivery. When he invited everyone to our house in California for Thanksgiving dinner, I wanted to maim him. Cooking for two is one thing, cooking for twenty when everyone is expecting the perfect meal, is a whole other game changer. I'm not embarrassed to say it. I've paid someone to cater our holiday dinner. Plus, I don't have time, even if I wanted to take on the task of feeding everyone.

"Maybe in high school, but my days of throwing the spiral are done with bare feet in the sand and Noah on the receiving end. I'm not looking to make a career under the pads."

"No, I think you're doing pretty well with what you have going on now. Let's talk about your upcoming wedding."

A sense of dread washes over me. Not because I'm worried about what Logan might think, but because I haven't done any planning. Elle and Paige picked out their own dresses. Noah ordered our invitations, but they're still in boxes because we don't have a guest list. My dress has been ready for at least a month and is still at the shop waiting for me to pick it up. The groomsmen don't have their suits. I ordered the flowers months ago and have honestly forgotten what they look like. We have nothing planned for a reception, nor have we booked the church for the actual ceremony. We haven't secured a minister or talked about our vows. My wedding is supposed to be in five weeks and I'm the most disorganized bride to ever walk the planet. I'm surprised Noah hasn't called the whole thing off.

"What do you want to know?" Probably where his invite is.

Logan leans forward and sets a small envelope down on the table with my Aunt Josie's name on it. "What's this?" I ask, turning it over and pulling out an RSVP card.

"I'm letting you know I'll be there."

"Um... I don't understand."

Logan looks at me oddly.

"What I mean is, I didn't send this out. How did you get it?"

He shrugs and stands, preparing to leave my office. "It came in the mail. See you after Thanksgiving." Logan leaves me in my office, holding this card with his name and the number of people attending. I flip it over, hoping for some more information, but there isn't anything.

THE ENTIRE FLIGHT TO CALIFORNIA, Noah ignored me. He pretended to sleep or acted so enthralled with the book he's reading that he couldn't be bothered to answer any of the questions I have about the reservation card Logan gave me earlier. I tried asking Elle, my mom, and Josie, but they all acted like they had no idea what's going on. Clearly, someone is up to something and whoever it is, needs to spill the beans.

Not far from our house is a private airfield. After we bought the house, Noah made friends with the guy, promised him some tickets to a few games in exchange for us being able to land the jet there. It's such a convenience, not having to deal with traffic, and once we land, we're home within minutes.

Noah pulls our SUV up to the curb, avoiding the garage. "What's going on?"

"Nothing, why?"

"Why aren't you pulling into the garage?"

"The door has been sticking. I'm not sure if Hank has fixed it yet." Hank, being the man we hired to manage the property while we're in Portland for the season. He makes sure everything's in working order, that the shrubs stay nice and trimmed, mows what little lawn we have, and the pool is clean and functioning. He'll stay on, even after we move here in February.

"Huh." I get out of the car, grab my bag and head toward the front door. I love this house and it's cute New England charm. When I reach the top of the stairs, I run my finger along the wood shingle. Who knew something like a cedar shingle would give a house so much character.

Inside, I go directly to our master bedroom. Noah and I haven't been able to spend much time here, but in a few months, all that will change. Unpacking quickly, I begin to wonder where Noah is. I call out for him, and nothing.

"Odd," I say to myself as I walk through the house. It's a bit chilly today, the glass walls are closed to keep the heat in, but the view is still as spectacular as ever. "Noah?" This time I yell, and he hollers back that he's downstairs. Of course, he is. He has a man cave down there.

I have to turn the lights on in the hallway, and again in the great room. As soon as they come on, my eyes barely have time to adjust before a cacophony of voices scream "Surprise!"

"Holy shit." I hold my hand over my chest to try and squash the rapid beating. "What is this?"

Noah comes toward me with a big smile on his face. "It's your bridal shower."

"My what?" That's when everything starts to come into focus. The room is decorated with white and silver bridal décor, there's a table full of presents, a cake and heaps of food, and the people that are here: my mom, sister, grandma, Yvie, Noah's family, and my sorority sisters.

Noah leans down and whispers into my ear, "Every bride deserves a party. Enjoy it."

"Did you do this for me?" Tears start to form in my eyes and I'm doing everything I can to stop from crying.

"It was a team effort."

My mom and Josie come over, followed by everyone else. One by one, I give everyone a hug. "How?" I ask my mom after I've greeted everyone and have had a moment to decompress.

"Josie and I, along with your sister and Betty Paige. Noah has helped with information when we asked. We realized that you're both so busy that you don't have time to plan a wedding." My mom reaches for my hand. "I know you want to get married at Christmas, and you will. We've taken care of everything. You and Noah just have to show up."

"Are you serious? You've taken care of everything?"

Both moms nod. "Noah has been sneaking us pictures of your wedding book. We've implemented everything. The groomsmen have their suits. As you know, the flowers are taken care of. The dads met with the caterers and DJ for the reception."

I can't hold back the tears any longer. My family has

taken care of everything to give me my dream wedding. I look around the room, it's filled people I love. Some of whom I haven't seen since graduation. Everyone is talking to each other, they're eating and drinking, waiting for me to join them.

Noah appears at my side and slides his arm over my waist as he kisses me on my cheek. He holds his lips there and whispers that he loves me. He truly does. Either that or he's trying to wife me up before one of the guys on the team asks me to marry him.

"Where are we getting married?"

"Where my parents did," Noah tells me. "At six p.m. I'm hoping you'll meet me there. I'll be the guy standing at the front, with your brother and my dad by my side, waiting for the love of his life to walk down the aisle with her dad by her side."

I turn and pull Noah into my arms. "I'll be there. I promise."

18

NOAH

*M*y hand slams down on my phone in a failed attempt to shut off the alarm blaring through the speaker. It's five in the morning and still very dark outside on Christmas morning. It's also the day the love of my life becomes my wife. Automatically, I reach for her even though I know she's across town, sleeping in her childhood bed. I think the tradition that the bride and groom can't spend the night before their wedding together is the dumbest thing ever, especially when the couple already lives together. Someone please tell me why I'm waking up on Christmas morning without my girl?

As slowly as possible I start to get out of bed. My body is sore. My aches have aches. My bare feet touch the hardwood floor and I shiver, already missing the warm California sun and the mild weather of Portland.

Dressing quickly, I sneak out of my parents' house. Instead of driving, I jog to my destination. I figure I might as well get a workout in while I can because today is going to be nothing but eating and drinking. I'm going to need a vacation from Christmas.

Twenty very cold minutes later, I'm climbing up the trellis and onto the roof of the porch to the James' home. I haven't done this in years, but today calls for a little daredevil action. I don't want to wait until Peyton has had Christmas with her family until I can see her. Last night was torture. Almost as bad as when we're on a road trip and I know she's down the hall, sleeping in another room. I tried to convince our employer that Peyton and I should share a room, but they weren't buying it.

Last night I texted her and suggested she leave her window unlocked, telling her that if she were a good girl, Santa would pay her an early morning visit. Thankfully, she did. It takes a little effort to get the window up, but once it does, I slip in and close it quietly.

My girl is lying there like an angel, the comforter covering her right up to her chin. Her long dark hair spreads out over her pillow, waiting for me to run my fingers through it. I can't believe that by the end of the night she's going to be my wife. She's the only one I want to have children with, to grow old with. Right now I'm the luckiest guy in the world because I'm marrying the woman that my dreams are made of. Life doesn't get any better than this.

Kicking off my shoes, I pull back her comforter and slide in next to her, pressing into her backside. "Hey, baby," I whisper into her ear.

I wait for her to respond. To acknowledge that I'm here.

Nothing.

"Baby." I rest my hand under her shirt. She tenses. "P, I'm here."

She moans, but it's not that happy to feel you behind me kind type. It's the leave me alone, I'm sleeping type.

"Okay, I'll just hold you." I situate behind her, but she moves and tries to push me away. "Peyton, seriously."

"You know, for knowing me all my life, you would think you'd be able to tell us apart by now."

Before I can comprehend what's going on, someone's giggling behind me and Peyton – no strike that – Elle is sitting up in bed. I jump out quickly and stand in the middle of the room while the twin terrors laugh uncontrollably.

"Did you seriously twin me on my wedding day?" I ask the both of them. My soon-to-be-wife nods while her sister looks rather pissed.

"I can't believe you thought I was Peyton."

"Why wouldn't I?" I throw my hands up. "You're in her bed and when it's dark, you look just like her. I can't believe the both of you did this to me." I sit down on the edge of Peyton's bed, which is actually Elle's bed. For as long as I can remember, Peyton has always been on the left-hand side of the room.

"It was her idea." Elle points at Peyton, who feigns shock, causing me to shake my head.

As if this morning can't get any worse, their bedroom flies open, and Harrison is standing in the doorway. "Are you sneaking into my daughter's room?"

"Um..." I stand, unsure what the hell I'm supposed to do right now. He stalks toward me and for the first time since I've known him, I can easily say, I'm a bit terrified.

"Do you think because you're marrying my daughter that gives you the right to come through her window? To come into my home without my knowledge?"

I take a few steps back, but he keeps coming forward. Neither Peyton nor Elle are saying anything, and I'm starting to wonder how I'm supposed to get out of this.

"Oh, for the love of all things holy, Harrison. Leave Noah alone," Katelyn says from the doorway. She loves me. She has to. I'm her godson and she's my mom's best friend.

Harrison glares at me. My heart is about to fall into my stomach. I think I'm going to be sick. Never in my life, have I been in this situation. The room is eerily quiet while Harrison stares me down. I'm tempted to remind him... oh hell, I don't know what I can remind him about. He's right, I shouldn't be sneaking in through the window, but all I wanted to do was wake up on Christmas morning with Peyton. I really don't think that's too much to ask, especially considering we're about to be married. The tension in the room is palpable. I swallow hard and open my mouth to say something, but nothing, not even a squeak comes out.

Harrison stands tall and slowly sticks his hand out toward me. My eyes go from his to his hand, back to his eyes, and finally around the room. "Welcome to the family. I've always wanted to bust someone in the girls' room, so thank you for making my Christmas morning memorable."

Everyone in the room starts laughing. Everyone, that is, except for me. I don't find this funny at all. I don't even care about being caught by Harrison. What I care about is that I touched Elle. That's what bothers me the most.

"I'm going to go down and make a pot of coffee," Katelyn tells the room. Everyone leaves, except for Peyton. Elle closes the door behind her, giving us some privacy.

"That was mean."

"It was meant to be funny," she says, climbing out of bed and coming to me. Her hands start on my chest with

148

one over my rapidly beating heart, while the other moves to my hair. "I'm sorry."

"I touched your sister, Peyton. I would never—"

She stops my words with a deep, lingering kiss. "I know. I know you would never do anything to hurt me, Noah."

"I wouldn't. I love you so damn much."

Peyton doesn't return the sentiment. Instead, she goes to the desk and pulls open the drawer. "Tonight, we're going to be husband and wife, which is the best gift we could give each other. But, I saw this one afternoon, not long after we moved to Portland. I was walking around aimlessly, questioning everything that I knew."

She sets the small package into my hand. "Open it."

"Don't you want to wait for later?"

Peyton shakes her head.

I unwrap the box with such urgency one would think I've never opened a present before. Lifting the lid of the box reveals a black, industrial style watch. Peyton takes it out for me and turns it over. "What does it say?" I ask her.

She smiles softly. "You are my light, my happy, my everything. Today starts our forever." My hand covers the watch, holding it in her hand. She rises to kiss me. It's soft and perfect. "Merry Christmas, my love."

"Merry Christmas."

QUINN AND NOLA, who both slept through the earlier commotion, finally woke and joined us for breakfast. And because Betty Paige is the youngest, our clan will celebrate Christmas at my parents. Harrison volunteered to drive everyone over, but Katelyn nixed the idea, telling him that once Christmas is deemed over, it's wedding time and the women had places to be.

I thought about running back to my parents or riding with Katelyn, fearful that Harrison would try to kill me. Unfortunately, Katelyn's car was full, mostly taken up by a certain dress that I can't wait to see, and that left me with my previous two choices. Thankfully, Peyton's riding with me and I know Harrison will be on his best behavior.

At my parents', my dad hands me a beer the second I walk in the door, JD pats me on the back, telling me I've earned my stripes. They're both laughing and telling me it's about time I got my balls busted by Harrison. I'm so happy everyone thinks this is a laughing matter. I almost crapped my pants.

"Let's open presents," Betty Paige hollers at everyone and Eden seconds the statement.

"Why so eager?" I ask her, sitting down next to her on the floor.

"It's your wedding day, silly brother. We all have to get our hair did."

"Done," I correct her.

Paige rolls her eyes. "Missy Elliot says did so it's did. Geesh, Noah."

"Noah, sometimes I wonder whether you're cool or not," Eden chastises.

JD walks by and flips Eden's hair, pissing her off. She swats at her dad. Eden is a feisty one, and often battling with JD over the simplest of things.

"My bad." It seems like my day isn't starting off at all like I had hoped. Peyton comes into the room, hands me a plate of food, and sits down next to me. "We just ate, babe."

"It's Christmas food. I can't say no."

Who am I to argue with that logic? I balance the plate on my knee, giving us both easy access. Everyone else comes into the room. My dad's wearing a Santa hat. He's done this every year since he came back into our lives.

"Where's Ben?" he asks.

"With his mom, he'll be over later. We don't have to wait for him." Elle tells us. It's a bit sad he's the only one not here, but I get it. Honestly, I'm surprised that Nola didn't go home to be with her family, but I'm sure the wedding put a monkey wrench in everyone's plans.

My dad starts sorting the presents. There's so many under the tree that they're stacked against the wall. Most of them are for Betty Paige, and as her pile grows, my mom blurts out that once the grandbabies start coming, Paige is getting fewer presents.

"Don't tease me, Mommy."

"Bite your tongue, Mother," I add. "At least let Peyton and I enjoy being married before we start having babies." I lean over and kiss Peyton on the cheek, and whisper in her ear, "Unless you want a baby sooner." She shakes her head slightly, giving me my answer. We both know we want children, we just haven't said when. I think my mom tends to forget that Peyton is still young, and her career is just starting. We have time. Still, the look on my mom's and Katelyn's face tells me they're eager to be grandmas.

Once all the presents are handed out, we go one by one, opening a gift. With this many people, it takes forever but allows us to see what everyone is getting. When Peyton picks my gift to open, I turn all my attention toward her. She unwraps the box carefully lifting the lid.

Her hand instantly covers her mouth as she says my

name quietly. Nestled in the tissue paper is a framed photo of the both of us. We're about seven and twelve. I don't know who took it, but they captured Peyton looking at me while I pushed her hair behind her ear. I don't even remember the day, but to have proof that I've loved her forever is pretty damn special.

Underneath this frame is another. The picture is of Peyton, Mason, and me. This was taken at the last Thanksgiving we had with Mason. It had been raining for days, so the ground was saturated, but that didn't stop us from going outside and playing football. Mason has his arms around us, dirt covering our faces and jerseys, but we're smiling. We're happy.

"Noah, where did you find these?" Katelyn is kneeling before her daughter, looking at the photos.

"In a box, in the attic here. I found them earlier this summer when we were visiting."

"I'm going to need a copy of these," she says.

"Me too," my mom adds.

"Thank you," Peyton says with tears in her eyes. "Thank you so much for loving me."

Again, I'm doing what I've always done, and push her hair behind her ear. "I don't know what my life would be like if I didn't love you."

"Me neither."

"Save it for your vows," JD yells. We laugh, and as I look around everyone is wiping away their tears. I take a deep breath and try to calm my emotions or at least save them for later when I promise to devote the rest of my life to the girl sitting next to me.

19

PEYTON

$\mathcal{I}$ don't know where I would be if it weren't for the women in my life. The salon in Beaumont is closed due to my bridal party and as small as it is, the space is filled. Still, everyone I know is getting their hair done, or did, according to Paige. My sister is playing bartender and making sure the champagne is flowing freely and Eden has her phone plugged into the speaker system and is currently honing her DJ'ing skills.

The best part – everyone is laughing. There's laughter, and laughter is good. It feeds the soul. They're smiling, they're happy. All while I'm trying to hold it in. The last thing I want to do is cry, but I'm pretty emotional right now. As I stare at my family through the mirror, I'm trying to find the words to thank them for being my support system, my best friends, for holding my hand and never giving up on me after the accident. I want to tell them that if it weren't for their love and guidance, I wouldn't be the woman I am today.

Words escape me though. Earlier today, Christmas was poignant. The gift from Noah, even though he's given me so much over the past couple of years, was exceptional. I know the ring he'll slip on my finger this evening will mean more to me than anything, but having those photos of us, to look at and cherish them until the end of time means so much to me. I don't know if I'll ever find a way to properly express how I feel about him. Telling him I love him doesn't seem to do my feelings justice, and while actions speak louder than words, sometimes I feel like I can't hug him tight enough or hold him long enough to show him how I feel.

I meant the words I put on his watch with every fiber of my being... He *is* my light. I can't explain it. He guided me away from a darkness that wanted to consume me, to eat me alive. He fought for me when I couldn't fight for myself. He loved me when I was broken, when he broke me and did everything he could to put the pieces back to make me whole. To make *us* whole.

"I can't believe you're marrying Noah Westbury." I look at the stylist through the mirror and smile. "Noah and I graduated high school together. He was *the* catch. Everyone wanted him."

And I had him the whole time.

"Yes, I remember. Girls were always at his house, calling him, following him around."

"But he rarely paid attention."

That's because he was in love with me.

"Some thought he was gay," she says, which causes me to laugh.

"Sorry, I didn't mean to move."

"No worries, I probably shouldn't have said that. I think those who did were probably rejected by him." She smiles softly and goes back to work, pinning half of my curls up. Noah loves my long hair and being that it's winter I want to keep most of it down. "Christmas weddings are so beautiful."

"I agree."

Mom comes over with a big grin on her face. "Oh Peyton, you're going to be such a beautiful bride." She kisses my cheek, smelling of champagne.

"Thanks, Mom. Hey, Elle, maybe chill out on giving Mom so much to drink."

Mom scoffs and waves my comment off as she goes back to the other gals. Aunt Josie and Betty Paige are getting manicures, Eden and Elle are getting pedicures, and it seems that Jenna and my mother are hitting the bottle.

"You're pretty lucky," the hairdresser says.

"Why do you say that?"

She nods toward Josie. "She's Noah's Mom, right?" I nod. "Yeah, she came in one day and asked about services. When she told us it was going to be on Christmas, we all passed."

"What changed your mind?"

"She told us your story and everything you've been through. She sat in here for an hour after we closed, talking about Noah and his love for you. I was the first one to say yes, the other girls followed quickly."

"Thank you. I know working on Christmas Day isn't the best way to spend the time."

"No, but helping a bride look her best for her fairy tale wedding is a pretty good reason to skip dinner at my in-laws."

By the time I've been buffed, polished, had my makeup applied, I'm on edge. My team is doing everything they can to keep my nerves calm on the ride over to the church. The limo pulls around the back, but not before I see so many people walking in.

"People came," I say as I look out the window. My mom holds my hand, squeezing it lightly.

"Everyone RSVP'd, Peyton," Josie says.

"Everyone?"

She nods. That means there are over five hundred people cramming into that church, on Christmas night. That means people gave up time with their families, to watch ours become one.

"Don't cry, sweetie." My mom pats my leg. Too bad her words make me want to cry even more now.

Once the limo driver opens the door, we rush inside. In the small chamber room, my dress is hanging, suspended in mid-air, waiting for me to slip into it.

"Jenna pressed it one more time before she and Eden started their duties," Mom tells me. Jenna oversees the guest book, while Eden hands out programs. Jimmy is an usher. The perfect job for a man like him, escorting women to their seats. No doubt cracking jokes as he walks them down the aisle.

I go over to my dress and touch the silky fabric. In terms of design, this is a simple gown. It's perfect for me.

"I have your something new," Betty Paige says. She hands me a small blue box tied in white ribbon. "It's from Noah."

I look at her questioningly before pulling on one of the ribbons. Inside the box, is another box. She helps me pull it out and holds it while I flip the top open. Nestled on top of velvet is a diamond tennis bracelet, set in platinum.

"If you look underneath each piece or whatever you call them, it says Noah and Peyton," Paige tells me. I do as she says and flip the bracelet over once I have it out of the box. Sure enough, there's a tiny letter on each bracket, and enough to spell out our names.

"Wow, I'm lost for words."

"He loves you, P. And so do I. I'm so happy that you're going to be my sister." Paige and I hug. When we part, she helps me slip it onto my wrist.

"I have your something blue." Josie steps forward. I open the bag and pull out a blue garter.

"Oh boy," I say as I let it hang from my finger. "I have a feeling the reception is going to get a bit rowdy tonight." Everyone laughs.

"And I have your something borrowed." Mom holds out her hand, there's a set of small diamond earrings resting in her palm. "I know we live this glamorous life, where we have everything, but these were a gift from your father and I thought that maybe you'd like to wear them today."

The tears I've been holding back arrive in full force. Elle's dabbing my face and cursing up a storm, while I hug my mom. "I'd be honored," I tell her through my tears. I always knew weddings could be touching, but I guess when you have a family like mine, who've been through what we have, there's even more reason to cry when you're supposed to be happy.

After my mom, Josie, and Paige leave, it's just my sister and me. We hug for a long time. It doesn't matter that we haven't lived together in years or that we've gone our own ways, this is a turning point for us.

"Are you changing your last name?" she asks as she helps put the diamond studs into my ears.

"I am. I've thought about it for a long time and being a Westbury feels right. Professionally, I'll stay James, but I can't wait to be Peyton Westbury and have it be real. Have it be mine."

Elle smiles and brushes a stray curl over my shoulder. "Noah's one lucky guy."

"I'm the lucky one, Elle. I almost lost him."

"That would've never happened." Her voice is strong and confident. She's so much stronger than I am.

My sister helps me into my dress and hands me my bouquet just as there's a knock on the door. She stands there with her hands on my shoulders, her smile is soft. "Daddy... I mean, our father, he would've been so proud of you, Peyton. I know I am. Being your sister is the best part of my life."

"Elle..."

"No, don't cry." She pulls a tissue from her pocket. Of course, she would buy a gown with pockets. "You deserve every happiness, and I'm so happy that it's Noah who gets you for the rest of your life because you're pretty freaking awesome."

"Thank you." I want to tell her that it's okay to refer to our father as daddy. I certainly have and would never think badly of her if she did. I touch the earrings and smile. "I have him with me, always."

"He's here now. I can feel him. He wouldn't miss this day for anything."

Her words give me pause. I've done everything I can to block him out. Not because I don't love him, but felt consumed by his presence, and I needed to focus on Noah and the life we're trying to build.

There's a knock on the door. My sister presses her forehead to mine. "I love you, P."

"I love you more," I tell her.

She smiles and inhales deeply before turning her attention to the door. "Come in," she says.

Our dad and Quinn walk in, both dressed handsomely in the suits I picked out. "Wow," Dad says. "Just wow."

"She's gorgeous," Elle adds. "The perfect bride."

Quinn comes over and whispers. "Say the word and we ride away on my bike. I can take him out, if need be." I chuckle.

"He's your best friend."

"You're my sister. Marriage will never ever change that."

"I love you, Quinn."

"I love you more," he says, kissing me on the cheek. He leaves with Elle, giving me a minute with our dad.

"You up for this?" I ask him.

He nods, and his lips go into a fine line. He's holding back, keeping his emotions in check. "I can stand here and say a bunch of stuff about how beautiful you are, how strong and resilient you've been, and how lucky Noah is, but you know this already. The only thing I want to say is thank you."

"For what?"

"For trusting me when you were five. For letting me in. For calling me Dad. For being one of the best things to ever happen to me."

"Daddy," I choke out over a sob.

"Don't cry, baby girl. You've got one hell of a man waiting for you upstairs, and as much as it pains me to let you grow up, I'm supposed to walk you down the aisle and give you away to him."

"He loves me."

"I know he does. Shall we?" He holds his arm out for me to take. In the hall, Elle is waiting for us. She picks up the train of my dress and carries it as we climb up the stairs. Liam and Paige are there when we reach the vestibule. She squeals with excitement, but Liam, he wipes a fallen tear from his face. It's not lost on me that this was where we said goodbye to my father, where Liam and I bonded instantly. That's not why I chose this church. This is where life began for our families, where the bridge became strong. Whether Liam knows it or not, he's the patriarch that keeps us going.

Jimmy opens the doors to the church and I can hear everyone turn in their seats, hoping to get a glimpse. Liam and Paige walk down the aisle first, followed by Quinn and Elle. I can easily say there will be no bridal party hook-ups happening at my wedding.

The music changes and my dad's voice sings out over the loudspeaker. I smile at his reaction. While the moms may have planned everything, I made a few changes. This being one of them. Years ago, he made a demo for Elle and me, our own songs and how he felt about us. I chose to have it playing now, as opposed to later, because he wanted to pick the song we danced too. Either way, I win.

We slowly turn the corner. Everyone stands, a few people gasp, but my eyes are focused only on Noah. Quinn whispers something in his ear and he smiles. He smiles like he's never smiled before. Each step I take, it's slow. I'm the tortoise trying to beat the rabbit in a race right now, and my prize is waiting. After what seems like an eternity walking down the aisle, I'm finally face-to-face with my groom, who looks really hot in his suit.

"Who gives this bride-to-be with this man?"

My dad clears his throat. "Her mother and I do," he says right before he kisses me softly on my cheek.

"Holy fuck, Peyton, you're beautiful."

My eyes go wide at Noah's little outburst. I chance a look at the minister who shrugs. "At least it's holy." Everyone in church laughs.

Noah and I look longingly into each other's eyes while the minister talks about our life, the love we share, and what our future holds. Truthfully, I'm not listening. The only thing I want to do is hear the minister announce us husband and wife, kiss my groom and get to the party where I can dance the night away with the man of my dreams.

"Noah, your vows?"

Noah grins. "Peyton, it seems like all I do is tell you how much I love you. I think part of me is scared that one day I'll wake up and this will all be a dream. The other part of me doesn't want you to forget or ever wonder if I don't. If there's ever a day that I don't tell you, kick me, because you deserve to be told every single day of your life. Few people can say they met the love of their life at the age of five. I can. Being in your life has been the single greatest moment of mine. Being your husband is going to be the best part of life yet. Tonight, in front of our family and friends, in this church on Christmas, I vow to you to be the best husband, friend, and father to our children that I can be, and to be the man that you deserve. I love you, Peyton."

Elle hands me a tissue so I can dab at my tears. I smile at Noah and take a deep breath. "I didn't know what I was going to say until this moment. You've seen the worst of me, even on my best days, and never judged me. Never asked me to change. You only offered guidance, understanding, and help, and for that I love you. For as long as I can remember, you've been in my life. Every memory I have, you're there. You're present. You know what I'm thinking before I do. You know what I'm going to say before I can form a proper response. You hold my hand and let me jump first, never pushing. I am, who I am, because of you, and I could never imagine my life without you. Today, in front of our family and friends, I become your wife, your partner, and the woman who tells you when your plays are sloppy." Those final words earn some loud laughter from the people in attendance.

"Noah, you brought me back from the darkness and showed me what it's like to live. For that, I am forever grateful. I love you more than words can say, more than actions can show, and being your wife is going to be the easiest thing I ever do."

"Well, I'm not sure there's a dry eye in the house," the minister says. "Now if we could have the rings."

Noah and I each take turns slipping our rings on each other's fingers and repeat our solemn vow.

"By the power vested in me, I now pronounce you husband and wife. Noah, I think it's time to kiss your wife."

Noah doesn't have to be told twice, and neither do I. What I'm not expecting is for my husband to pull me to him and dip me down as he kisses me. "You're my wife," he whispers against my lips before helping me stand on my feet.

"Ladies and gentlemen, I am proud to introduce, Mr. and Mrs. Noah Westbury."

Our hands go up, much to the delight of everyone in the church. Noah kisses me again before we walk down the aisle. When we get to the end, we turn and look at our family and friends. Someone yells that we have to kiss, and that's when I look up and find a sprig of mistletoe hanging above us.

"Can't leave a girl hanging, Westbury."

"Never," he says as he pulls me into his arms.

Never can't be quantified, and I like that because I want this moment to last forever. Being his wife, it's a dream come true.

THE END...

... until Liam & Harrison become grandpas!!

ABOUT HEIDI MCLAUGHLIN

Heidi McLaughlin is a New York Times, Wall Street Journal, and USA Today Bestselling author of The Beaumont Series, The Boys of Summer, and The Archers.

Originally, from the Pacific Northwest, she now lives in picturesque Vermont, with her husband, two daughters, and their three dogs.

In 2012, Heidi turned her passion for reading into a full-fledged literary career, writing over twenty novels, including the acclaimed Forever My Girl.

When writing isn't occupying her time, you can find her sitting courtside at either of her daughters' basketball games.

Heidi's first novel, Forever My Girl, has been adapted into a motion picture with LD Entertainment and Roadside Attractions, starring Alex Roe and Jessica Rothe, and opened in theaters on January 19, 2018.

Don't miss more books by Heidi McLaughlin! Sign up for her newsletter, or join the fun in her fan group!

Connect with Heidi!
www.heidimclaughlin.com

LOST IN YOU SERIES

Lost in You

Lost in Us

THE BOYS OF SUMMER

Third Base

Home Run

Grand Slam

THE REALITY DUET

Blind Reality

Twisted Reality

SOCIETY X

Dark Room

Viewing Room

Play Room

THE CLUTCH SERIES

Roman

STANDALONE NOVELS

Stripped Bare

Blow

Sexcation

Santa's Secret

Christmas With You

COMING SOON

See You Again - June, 2019